SHADOWS OF RHAPTA

RHAPTAVERSE CHRONICLES BOOK 2

LILY SKYY

Shawdows of Rhapta
Copyright © 2024 by Lily Skyy
www.LilySkyy.com

First Edition: August 2024

ISBN 978-1-962071-78-9 (ebook)
ISBN 978-1-962071-79-6 (paperback)

Published by Books to Hook Publishing, LLC.
www.BooksToHook.com

CONTENTS

CHAPTER 1
AN UNEASY ALLIANCE

For the third time that day, Kareem's heart was in his throat as he tried to approach his team.

In the dining hall, he grabbed dinner early, moving to sit where Zara ate alone during the evening meal. He even tried to creep up quietly, hoping that if he sat, she would at least refuse to leave.

He was wrong.

As soon as he set his tray down, Zara got up. He went to call for her but instead stopped.

He sighed.

It was to be expected, he supposed, given how the last few weeks had gone.

A heavy tension clung to Kareem as he moved through the days that passed since his team's confrontation back in Toronto. Thoughts of SPE and everything he had learned trailed him like a shadow as he sat through his classes, did his training, and worked on the chores he and the others were given as punishment for what they had done. To Kareem, it was almost strange that the world around them marched on, seemingly unchanged, while his head swam with the memories of the ubir who attacked them. Memories of that strange woman from SPE. Memories of what the ubir had told them—that their mentor, Neelan, was in trouble and *humans* were holding Anunnaki captive. Every corner Kareem turned, every room he entered, a sense of unease followed, making his skin prickle.

Several weeks had passed since he and the others were scolded and punished by Savar. Several weeks since they won the skirmish, but they had gotten their reward of going on their first unsupervised assignment taken away from them. Kareem supposed they should consider themselves lucky not to be expelled for what they had done—what they had *seen*—but as they dodged the everwatchful gaze of the guards that seemed to follow them wherever they went, he got the feeling Savar and Zaid thought it was better to keep an eye on them rather than banish them from the House. Reluctantly, they had been laying low, wearing the masks of exemplary Venari trainees, burying their frustrations and behaving themselves, pretending the memories of Neelan and the other captured Anunnaki were merely fleeting figments of their imaginations. Because that was what Savar wanted.

It was a matter of survival.

Kareem wasn't about to challenge destiny a second time. Stepping out of line again, sneaking out of Rhapta to search for Neelan and these SPE fools, would spell their banishment. He wanted to graduate from training and become a Venari quicker than anyone else had, but how could he make that dream a reality if he kept breaking the rules? By now, he should already have one unsupervised assignment under his belt. He won the skirmish. But his actions took away that opportunity from him, despite Kareem only wanting to help save Neelan.

Rhapta didn't feel the same to Kareem anymore. It had turned from a cherished haven into a gilded cage. His team sensed it too—the inescapable feeling of Savar's scrutiny. As much as they yearned to find Neelan and unravel SPE's mysteries, they were forced to act as though nothing was wrong. Being expelled was one thing, but leaving Rhapta and getting caught would get them imprisoned. None wished to entertain that chance.

Kareem thought he and his team were terrible actors. Even when remaining in Venari training depended on their ability to resume life as though it hadn't changed, they could hardly do it. Every movement through the halls that he and his friends made was on short, hurried footsteps. They scuttled between their classes, heads down and glances furtive as their eyes darted to meet each other over books or around corners. Kareem would try to catch their attention for a study group or for practice with combat up on the roof, but it was to no avail. Even though they were a team, it was as though they were all too afraid to be too near to one another, in case Savar saw and assumed they were up to no good.

Ovi, Zara, and Binita no longer responded to Kareem as their leader.

While others grew more interested in him because they heard a rumor about him being up to no good, his teammates parted around him as though he were invisible. Kareem noted the deteriorating sense of "team" with two lenses. First, he strongly felt that, as their leader, he needed to say something about it.

Second, as a person, he felt the loss of his team's closeness, like a toothache. He often lay awake at night, worrying about them and where they stood.

It had taken them so long to work together.

Now, they were falling apart.

Kareem knew that something had to be done to alleviate the tension before it broke them apart entirely and before it took too much away from the passion they had once felt around rescuing Neelan. Every day that passed, he watched the desire to do something fade from his friends, and Kareem felt like, without any action, they would settle into the tempting lull of inaction.

Neelan and the missing Anunnaki couldn't handle that.

Kareem couldn't handle it either. Despite the lack of trust he now felt toward Savar, the Venari leader made Kareem the leader of his own team, and he had chosen him for a reason. That meant it was Kareem's responsibility to get himself and the others back on track. Since they turned the papers on SPE over to Savar, their momentum had dissipated. They were being watched. It made them feel stuck. Like they couldn't move forward. And the more time that passed, the more Kareem wondered if they were just afraid or if they no longer wanted to.

Kareem had been watching Ovi descend further into himself ever since he used his powers to hurt the ubir, Adonal, to protect Binita and stop him from killing her. Since then, Ovi had become a quiet shell of the roommate that Kareem had come to know. Binita and Zara became secretive and shy. They often looked Kareem's way but never directly spoke to him.

Tension.

Kareem lived it. He breathed it.

And he was sick of it.

It was when he was studying in the library, when Binita and Zara's whispers around the corner sounded more like the low hiss of snakes than an actual conversation, that Kareem decided it was finally time to make them listen. He shot up from his seat, walked around a bookcase, and approached the girls on his team.

Enough, he snapped at them. Zara's dark brown eyes shot him a sharp look, which instantly softened Kareem as guilt pooled in his stomach. *I'm sorry. It's just that we can't keep doing this.*

Doing what? Zara's gaze was piercing.

Running around like mice hiding from a cat. Kareem folded his arms and tried not to glare back at her. *We haven't been expelled. It's time to try and find those phones. We need to break into that office, not act like nothing happened. Too much time has passed. We're losing our motivation. But Neelan still needs us.*

Zara snorted. *I'm pretty sure acting like nothing happened is our only course of action at this point. I'm sorry, but I don't want to get sent home.*

Me neither, Binita added softly. *I can't see any way that pursuing the phones wouldn't lead to us getting kicked out.*

It was your *idea, Binita!* Kareem snapped. *Neelan deserves our commitment.*

Yeah—and we can't help Neelan if we're expelled, *idiot*, Zara practically shouted. They all glanced around, hopeful that their words hadn't drawn any extra attention.

We can't just do nothing, either, Kareem added in a whisper once the coast was clear.

Binita's face softened. *I know, Kareem. I want to find him, too. But… it's too risky. We did what we could. For now, that has to be enough.* Both Binita and Zara turned, effectively dismissing him.

Kareem refused to accept it. He remained where he stood, thinking it over. Since handing over their research on SPE and getting confined to their room for over three days, they had been so completely compliant that they could have been the archetype for a Venari student. The other students and teams clearly thought something was amiss; several times now, they had teased Kareem and his friends for their newfound love of the rules. While Kareem was definitely sick of that, he also knew that it was necessary. But not their new, permanent dispositions. Staying compliant would not get them anywhere.

It was only supposed to serve as a mask they wore until Savar grew less wary and turned the other cheek. Then, they were supposed to get right back to figuring out what was happening inside Rhapta and outside of it.

Kareem checked around again to be sure they were still alone in the library, and then he leaned in toward them.

We can't just give up. You know it. I know it. We just have to be smarter. If Savar and the others won't take the threat of SPE seriously, we either need to find out why, or we need to find out how to get to Neelan. Either way, it's been enough time. We've been too quiet, he said with a final meaningful glance at both girls. *We have to find him.*

Binita and Zara exchanged glances. *I think we need more time,* Zara argued, tossing her glossy dark locks over her shoulder, sending a wave of slightly dizzying vanilla perfume wafting through Kareem's nostrils. *We don't have any idea what we're getting into or how it's being handled. We need to come up with the answers to some of our questions before we just jump into something.*

No, Kareem said emphatically. *We've had plenty of time.*

Binita sighed, wrapping one of her thick, dense curls around her finger as she contemplated. *What do you have in mind?*

Wait, seriously? Zara asked her, her eyes narrowing.

Kareem grinned at Binita, glad he could count on her. A small flame of hope lit inside him. *Meet me in the empty study room by the back music room. For a... study group,* he said with a waggle of his eyebrows that he hoped alleviated some of the weirdness between them. Zara rolled her eyes, but Binita nodded.

Good choice, she said to Kareem. *No one will be there after dark.*

So, we're suddenly back on? Zara asked, a tinge of whininess in her tone.

Thanks, Kareem said.

Binita gave him a small, hesitant smile. *You'd better go and let Ovi know as well.*

Kareem nodded, then slipped off to find Ovi. Putting their quest in motion again felt like the right move. Ovi was in their small, plain room, sitting hunched at his desk, one of the only few pieces of furniture that filled the space. They each had a desk, a bed, and some shelving. Even though they'd been at the

House since the end of August, and it was now nearing the end of the year, neither had done anything to spruce up the place and make it feel more like home. They had been instructed before their arrival to bring little with them. They had to learn to own few possessions—that was part of the life of a Venari. The wood chair creaked softly every time he moved, but his head was bent over his book, exactly where Kareem suspected he would be.

Hey, Ovi, Kareem said.

With his back turned, Ovi gave him a small wave. It was more acknowledgment than Binita or Zara had given him, so Kareem felt appreciative of the attention.

Kareem paused, his eyes glued to his roommate. While he couldn't quite put his finger on it, he knew something was wrong. He and Ovi had talked a lot after they returned to Rhapta, and the same fear that Kareem had sensed in Ovi's words then was present now. His roommate was tense, quiet, and seemed even more affected by the rigidity that dominated all of them.

Telling Ovi the time had come to resume their search should have been the easiest thing. Out of the four of them, Ovi and Kareem had the strongest connection. They were roommates and friends, and he knew that Ovi would have his back no matter what.

So, his hesitation felt wrong.

Neither, however, did Kareem want to disturb Ovi. He still hadn't fully understood what Ovi had done to the ubir back in Canada, and Kareem was fairly certain that Ovi didn't understand it either. Adonal had gone stiff as a board when Ovi touched him with his bare hands. For a moment after he collapsed, Kareem had wondered if Ovi killed him. But then he saw the ubir scarcely breathing. Still, it made Kareem curious; could Ovi kill someone with his ability if he didn't hold back?

Ovi using his ability that day was the elephant in the room, and some of the inertia Kareem had built up around finding the phones seemed to bleed off. He looked at the back of his room-mate's head, took a breath, and blew it out.

Study room. Tonight. He cautiously kept his eyes trained on him. *It's time.* He didn't miss that Ovi's shoulders tensed at his words. The moment stretched, rippling with so many things that they hadn't said.

Finally, Ovi turned. *Did you tell Zara and Binita?*

Kareem nodded in response.

Ovi's face was inscrutable as he turned back. *Okay. I'm finishing up. I'll meet you there.*

Sounds good, Kareem replied with a false sense of confidence. Ovi's lack of response felt not only disheartening but dismissive. Ovi clearly didn't want to expand on how he was feeling, and Kareem might have been dying to ask, but it was clear Ovi was not in the same mood to share as he had been a few weeks ago.

Kareem wavered. Should he ask? Should he let Ovi come to him when he was ready? He hesitated in the doorway, hoping his room-mate would give him a clue about what felt right.

Ovi didn't turn.

Kareem's stomach sank. However, he took the hint. He gently closed the door and, despite his anxiety about his roommate, walked down the hall.

He knew in his heart that it had been enough time for the fuss around their discovery to die down. They had done everything right. They had followed all of the rules. It was time to get those phones. They needed access to the information their scant internet could provide, and they needed it fast. They needed to be able to find where Neelan was and what SPE had to do with it.

It was definitely time to act.

Kareem only hoped that the others would feel the same way.

WHEN KAREEM FOUND the study room after dark, he glanced down the hallway to check for anyone nearby. Finding it empty, he slipped inside.

Binita, Zara, and Ovi were waiting for him.

Kareem greeted them. Zara looked angry, her arms folded in defiance. Binita looked tired. She had dark bags beneath her eyes, and they shaded her otherwise delicate face.

Ovi's drawn face was partially hidden in the shadows as he sat back in his chair. *Hey, Kareem*, he said quietly.

Kareem's heart pinched. *You good, Ovi?*

Ovi shrugged. *I'm okay. Got all that stuff done. Extra credit, some things on the side. We're here now, so I'm ready to hear what you've got. What's up?*

Zara and Kareem exchanged glances. Ever since Ovi's strange power had been revealed, he had been withdrawn and pensive. Zara raised an eyebrow, clearly implying that Kareem needed to do more to support Ovi.

Kareem shrugged. There was only so much he could do. Ovi wasn't willing to open up, so Kareem couldn't help what he didn't know. And it seemed with Ovi, they didn't know a great deal.

Kareem needed to rejuvenate the team's vigor without making them too upset. *It's been weeks. None of us got expelled. It's time to go after those phones so that we can figure out who SPE is and what they want. If Binita is right, they're still locked in that adviser's office in the Grand Hall.*

Zara's eyebrows shot up so quickly that Kareem was surprised they didn't cause a ripple of friction across her forehead. *That was weeks ago. You think they're still in there?*

We haven't exactly given them cause to think we know where the phones are, Kareem replied dryly.

They're still in there, Binita responded. *I saw them just the other day.*

Zara's hands flew up at her. *And you're just telling me this now?*

Binita shrugged. *It wasn't relevant until now. We were lying low. We didn't need to know then, and we need to know now. I saw the phones in the office when I was... when I was walking around.*

Do you walk that far often? Zara deadpanned.

I like to walk. I happened to be on a walk before breakfast, and I can confirm that they're still there.

Binita... Zara began, irritation clear in her tone.

Okay, Kareem interjected. *The phones are still there. We just need to break in and take them back.*

You don't think they'll notice they're missing? Zara snapped.

Not if we put some replacements in their place. The group turned to look at Ovi.

What do you mean? Binita urged.

The phones. We could just put replacements in there. They won't know the difference. It's not like they're checking the messages or logging in to them. Using phones in Rhapta is still such a new concept. Not everyone learned how they operate from the queen. And a lot of people still don't have an interest in technology, Ovi clarified.

Kareem blinked. *Where would we find decoy phones?*

Ovi hesitantly waved a hand. *I... I can handle that. I think.*

Kareem did not doubt that Ovi could do just that. Given his reflective nature the last few weeks, he was grateful to see Ovi volunteering now.

And breaking into the office? Zara asked.

Binita leaned forward, her eyes sparkling with her focus. *I think we need to get the dummy phones first. I'll work on the lock. They'll probably leave it unmonitored during Auraday anyway. I think that's the best chance we have of getting into the office undetected.*

They'll just leave it open? Zara asked. *Auraday is a big deal, but big enough to forget to lock an adviser's office?*

Binita nodded. *It happened last year, too.*

Okay. Kareem grinned. *We have a plan.*

We barely *have a plan,* Zara argued. She looked around, meeting Binita's eyes first and then Ovi's. Finally, she looked at Kareem.

Zara. He tilted his head at her. *You were just as angry about this a few weeks ago. You wanted to find our phones then. What's changed now?*

Her eyes darted away, but Kareem could see her bristling. Binita gently nudged her, and Zara sighed. *I can't be expelled.* We *can't be expelled,* she said with a glance around the group. *If we're expelled, any chance we have of finding Neelan is gone. Any chance we have at exposing SPE, at finding the kidnapped Anunnaki... it's all just gone. I'd rather have a small chance than no chance at all.*

I hear you, Kareem agreed with a nod. *But we won't get expelled. We owe Neelan and everyone to figure out what's going on. The decision is made.*

Ovi's mysterious connection to the dummy smartphones would take him some time, or so he said, and Kareem asked no further questions. Especially since Ovi seemed to come to life for the first time in weeks. Kareem was grateful for it. The day after meeting up in the study room, he even laughed at one of Kareem's lame attempts at a joke. Progress.

Now, they were only a few days away from the first part of their plan being complete. When they walked into the classroom for their regular meeting with Hessa, their combat trainer, Kareem paused.

A new face lingered in Kareem's usual spot.

Who is that? he blurted out, causing a traffic jam in the door-way. Hessa, standing by the door to greet the students as they entered with her hands behind her back and her braided hair hidden under her hood, eyed him severely.

He's new. A student added on special designation. Hessa's tone was dry. *Does that meet your approval?*

Kareem didn't answer. Instead, he began to approach the new addition to their class, studying him. He was tall and lanky in a way that suggested he was both not done growing and had not had enough to eat to fill the spaces between his long bones. His face was a touch on the long side, but his eyes glittered with an intellect that made Kareem's spine tingle. He slouched, his body covered in baggy clothing that had seen one too many seasons, but Kareem had the sense that he could move like lightning if the occasion called for it. The new boy's energy felt coiled, like even when inert, he contained the necessary force to explode at a moment's notice.

Kareem didn't like his expression. Nor did he care for the energy he gave off. It made him immediately suspicious. No, he was not satisfied by Hessa Darvish's answer.

Who are you? Kareem asked the boy. Suspicion came through clearly in his tone. He made no effort to hide it and instead folded his arms in an effort to seem even less friendly.

The other student's eyes glimmered. Kareem tensed, recognizing the insolence in his gaze. *Does it matter?* he sneered.

They don't teach manners where you're from? Kareem quipped. *I asked you a question.*

And I declined to answer. The other boy smirked.

Kareem drew up to his full height, though he was still a bit shorter than this menace before him. *Do you think that's going to get you anywhere here? You—*

Enough, Hessa cut through Kareem's next words as the rest of the class filed in and took their places. *That's enough. Ashar is beginning a little later in the term, but he is no more behind than you were on your first day.*

Kareem backed down, but barely.

Hessa nodded approvingly. *Good. Thank you. However, I suppose proper introductions are in order between you two. Ashar, this is Kareem. Kareem, Ashar.*

Neither boy made any movement after the introduction.

Hessa shrugged. *So be it. Kareem, welcome your new team member. Ashar, this is your team leader. You will be assigned to Kareem's team for the duration of your Venari training. You will not switch teams, and you will not be able to adjust any of your teammates. Figure it out,* she said with an arched eyebrow. *You have no other option.*

Quickly shifting gears, she turned back to the rest of the class, gave her usual instructions for the day, and then their daily training began.

Kareem and Ashar glared at each other. Kareem wanted to say something, the words stringing together in his mind, when movement caught his eye.

Quick!

Zara's voice pulled both of their attention, and Kareem barely had enough time to bring his hand up to grab one of the practice spears Zara tossed at them. To his mild satisfaction, he noted that Ashar flinched in a similar manner as he caught his own.

Zara stepped forward, twirling her spear. She smiled at Ashar. *I'm Zara. Your teammate,* she said with her hand stuck out. Ashar's smile spread like honey across his face.

Ashar, he nearly purred. *I guess that there is something good about being on this team after all.*

What's your deal? Kareem hissed at Zara, grabbing her arm and turning them both away from the new kid. She shot Ashar a glance over her shoulder.

I'm being friendly, she quietly told Kareem, an innocent lilt in her voice. *Isn't that something you wanted? A little "teammate bonding?"*

You don't even know him, Kareem snarled at her. *He just got here. He's hardly even a teammate.*

Zara shrugged. *Might as well start off on the right foot.* She turned back to Ashar. *How good are you at sparring?*

In response, Ashar twirled the practice spear in a swift movement. *Fair to middling,* he said with another slow smile directed at her.

Kareem's anger and frustration bubbled up. He stepped in front of Zara. *I'll be the judge of that.*

Ashar swiftly gestured like he was about to throw his spear at him, faking him out. When Kareem flinched, Ashar grinned.

Zara's giggle hit Kareem like a bomb. He spun and stared at her. *Really?*

Oh, come on. Lighten up. She smiled at him. *He's just having some fun.*

Kareem gave her a nasty look and then spun back to Ashar. *Defensive position,* he snapped.

Ashar stared at him. He stood, that relaxed tension coiled inside his muscles.

But he didn't move.

Defensive. Position, Kareem enunciated.

Still, Ashar didn't move.

You're not ready, Kareem said. *Get into a defensive position.*

Ashar smiled. *Why don't you try and make me?*

Kareem's patience snapped. He flew at Ashar, his spear at the ready, hurtling with far more energy than was necessary. He lifted the spear, holding it up to an attack position.

The air shifted. Kareem stumbled. Ashar blurred behind him, and he felt the solid whack of a wooden spear against his back. Kareem didn't have time to process the pain; without realizing it, he found himself on the ground.

Ashar danced away, his spear twirling.

Frustration and embarrassment burned through Kareem as he sat up. *You little...*

A hand appeared in front of Kareem's face, and he took it. Zara pulled him up, smiling.

What's so funny? Kareem grumbled.

I think we've just found a perfect new teammate.

Kareem's eyes narrowed as he watched Ashar square off with Ovi next.

Perfectly terrible, *maybe,* he thought to himself. *But perfect? Definitely not.*

CHAPTER 2

IN THE SHADOW OF DOUBT

Kareem began the next day relieved to have the time to train on the rooftop with his team.

Rooftop training wasn't new, necessarily. They had taken to training together at their secret spot weeks ago but had paused after returning from Canada and dealing with the scrutiny that followed. They had only resumed recently, and Kareem looked forward to the sessions. It reminded him that they were a team, and it gave them the opportunity to discuss the plan to get the phones and continue their search for Neelan.

He was in an excellent mood when he climbed the familiar wooden ladder hidden inside the supply closet on the second floor up to the roof. He had been the last one up this morning, having woken up to an empty room, surmising that Ovi must have already gone up.

The sound of physical exertion and practice weapons met his ears, confirming his theory, and he grinned. His team was as supportive of each other as they could possibly be. They were strong, smart, and they were coming back together around their goals. In just a few days on Auraday, a holiday where the city celebrated the magical connection the Anunnaki had with the Auras-tones, they would get the smartphones from Ovi and swap them out for the phones in the office in the Grand Hall. Then, they could get back onto the internet. They could find out what SPE was. They could—

Kareem froze.

There was an extra person training with his team on the roof.

What in the...?

At first, he couldn't place the additional body. Then, the person's thin frame and long face clicked.

Ashar.

Kareem stormed forward. He ignored Binita's squeak of surprise and grabbed Ashar by the collar. Kareem pushed him back, shoving him against one of the stone walls that rose in a turret from the roof. *What are you doing here?* he snarled.

Is that any way to greet your new teammate? Ashar smirked at him.

Kareem pushed harder. *New teammate? Absolutely not. You haven't earned that title or my trust.*

Oh, I don't think that matters all too much, Ashar said with that same smirk. *We're going to spend plenty of time together. Might as well start now.*

Not if I have anything to say about it, Kareem growled.

Zara pushed on Kareem's arm. *Let him go,* she snapped. *I invited him!*

You did what? Kareem's attention turned to Zara. He dropped his arms and turned to face her. *Why would you invite him?*

Zara glared at him. *He's on our team! You heard Hessa. Ashar is part of the team now, and he needs to train as part of the team.*

He's not *part of the team!* Kareem shouted. Around him, he felt Binita and Ovi grow still. Zara pursed her lips, grabbed Kareem by the wrist, and pulled him away from everyone so they could talk privately.

Why are you being so weird about this? Zara demanded, her arms crossed, her long braids swinging around her waist. *He's one of us. We need to make sure we can work together. Or did you forget you're also training to be a Venari? It isn't just running around and solving...* mysteries, Zara caught herself. Kareem's eyes darted to Ashar, who was watching them with interest.

I'm not just solving mysteries, he responded to Zara quietly. *But we don't know him. He could be anyone. He could be...* he trailed off. He wanted to say that Ashar could be a spy for SPE or a mole set by the administration to find out if they were going to break Savar's decree.

Zara nodded. *I know,* she said quietly. *But again. It would be far more suspicious to just leave him out, right?*

Kareem's teeth ground together so hard, he could feel it in his neck.

She was right. Of course she was.

Ashar didn't need to know everything. He wasn't part of their group. He hadn't been there when they had found the ubir or hid from SPE. He wasn't one of *them.*

But Zara had pointed out something that Kareem's pride wasn't acknowledging. Even if Ashar was sent by Savar and the others, they had to maintain their existing state of affairs. If it was a test, they had to pass. They couldn't afford to arouse suspicion, especially not now that they were so close to getting the phones back and getting back on track with the mission to rescue Neelan and find out more about SPE. Ashar might be a spy, but if he was, Kareem and the others couldn't let on that they knew who he was. Ashar was here to stay.

And Kareem had to deal with it.

Fine. Kareem cast a reluctant gaze over at Ashar. *You can train with us outside of classes here. On a conditional basis. Today. And if you screw up, you can never come back.*

Ashar bowed, a mocking gesture that made Kareem's teeth grind again. *Thank you, my lord, for this humble opportunity.*

Shut up and stand up, Kareem grunted. *Explain why you're so good with a spear.*

Ashar's eyes glinted with that same defiance that Kareem had begun to associate with him. *I'm just a naturally gifted, fearless leader. What can I say?*

You can say the truth. Kareem's response was stern. *No one is that good with a spear without practice.* He folded his arms and widened his stance. On the off chance that Ashar would try to fight him, he wanted to be ready.

He wouldn't be taken off guard this time.

Ashar's grin curled at the edges of his lips. *Ah, I am no mere no one.*

How did you come to be here? Binita asked as she stepped forward. Her voice broke the energy that had been building between Ashar and Kareem.

Special dispensation. Diplomatic immunity. A harrowing and noble journey, Ashar said as his smile widened. *Which version do you prefer?*

The. Truth, Kareem grumbled.

Ovi leaned on his spear. *At least show us how you did that move to Kareem yesterday.*

That, my dear new friend, I can certainly manage, Ashar said with another bombastic bow. With a twirl and flourish, he whipped his spear into an elaborate set of maneuvers that had Binita and Zara practically cooing with delight.

Ashar spent the next few minutes modeling some impressive spear work for the team. Binita, Zara, and Ovi all tried to copy the movements with varying levels of success. Ashar seemed patient enough with them. He pointed out errors in their movements or holds and offered feedback that was both actionable and clear. He did a good job of teaching, and Kareem had to admit that. However, he wasn't quite sold on Ashar. He was absolutely good at combat, and there was no denying that. Kareem, while still skeptical, saw the finesse in Ashar's movements as he darted and danced around on the rooftop.

When Ovi came to stand by Kareem, panting lightly, Kareem nodded tersely. *He's pretty good.*

He's really *good,* Ovi wheezed as he leaned on his spear. *I'm glad he's on our team. Maybe he could help with...*

Hush. Kareem's eyes darted toward where Ashar was correcting Binita's form. He could have sworn that Ashar's muscles tightened slightly. *Right now, I don't trust him. And neither should any of you. Not yet.*

Fine. Sure. Ashar was good at teaching. And he was good at combat. But there was still something off about him, and Kareem wished his other teammates could see it. Ashar's breezy persona and devil-may-care attitude seemed too carefully crafted. It was like he was constantly performing, and he shifted that performance based on his audience every time. Kareem had the feeling that every person Ashar met had a different impression of him. He'd be sweet and thoughtful if the situation demanded it, clever and witty to another group, all while maintaining that careful distance that kept everyone he met at arm's reach.

In short, he reminded Kareem of a conman. Someone who could blend in, a social chameleon, then escape just as quickly when the time called for it. Kareem thought there was a lack of honesty behind his movements. And while he couldn't prove it, he knew Ashar was pretending with them in some way. He didn't know why or how, but he had no doubt the real Ashar would be a very different experience than the one presented to them here. Who was the real Ashar, and why had he so suddenly appeared? Why was he training to be Venari?

And who wanted him here?

The day stretched, the crisp, cool morning slowly heating until the time came for the group to go to class. They stopped their off-side training for the day, drinking water and toweling off.

So, Ashar said to the group as he stretched. *What's the plan for Auraday next week?*

Kareem's stomach knotted, every one of his senses calling out in warning. *What do you mean?*

The school. Do they decorate? Celebrate? Any fun plans? Any plans that are more fun because they're not supposed to happen? What's the vibe around here on Auraday?

Well, Binita started, *from what I heard, there's the usual stuff that happens all over Rhapta. You know—decorations, baskets. But I also heard the kitchen is going to produce some of the best Auraday cakes in the city. I think one of them is almond. I wonder if it will be as good as my family's recipe... Anyway, I heard some of the teachers get really drunk at the feast and show off their abilities.*

That sounds cool. Ashar grinned. *Like what?*

The usual, Ovi responded with a casual wave of his hand. *It's the same everywhere. Sparks from the ones who have electricity, some telepathy, some telekinesis. I remember once, when I was little, I was out with my aunt and uncle celebrating, and one of the younger Venari kept stealing the hats off an older one with his telekinetic energy. It was actually pretty funny.*

Ashar laughed. *I bet that was a sight to see.*

I heard it was. Binita smiled. *My cousin told me all about it.*

And you? What are your abilities? Ashar surveyed the group.

More alarms blared in Kareem's head. Any Anunnaki should know that asking someone about their abilities was a little too familiar for a stranger to do. *Why do you want to know?*

Ashar shrugged. *We're a team. Isn't it important to know what a team can do?*

Important. Sure. But you don't just walk into a room and ask someone what their ability is.

Ashar's eyebrows arched upward. *Why not?*

It's rude, Kareem stated. *Seriously. Where'd you even come from? Do you have any manners at all?* While he hadn't quite meant for it to be an insult, he saw it land as one. Ashar's eyes hardened, their glimmer and shine dulling as he dropped his mischievous smile. Kareem wondered if *this* was who the real Ashar was. Not the lackadaisical stranger Kareem opened the roof's door in the floor to that morning. This person was stony. Angry.

Possibly dangerous.

The moment slipped away, and Ashar seemed to regain control of himself, his face smoothing into its usual mildly amused expression. With his mask back in place, he snorted. *Manners didn't matter in the slightest where I grew up. It didn't keep you fed, and often, they just took too damn long to bother with.*

That sounds rough, Binita said quietly.

Ashar's face changed again, and this time he looked at Binita with something that genuinely resembled gratitude. *Thank you*, he said with more sincerity than Kareem had thought him capable of. *It was not easy.*

If you're so eager to get into everyone's abilities, why not offer a summary of your own? Kareem interjected. *You show us yours, we'll show you ours.* It went without saying that Ashar would not hear about Ovi's abilities anytime soon, but Kareem was willing to sacrifice knowledge of his own power if Ashar was willing to give up his secret in good faith.

Ashar grinned again. *I think that the anticipation will be enough for me for now. I look forward to finding out more later. Come on. Let's get to class. And tell me more about these cakes,* he said with a charming smile at Binita. She rolled her eyes, a mischievous grin curling at the corners of her lips. *I'll tell you my secrets if you tell me yours.*

Zara stepped up, cutting off whatever Ashar was going to say next. *They're incredible. Have you had Auraday cake before?* She started to walk toward the ladder. Ashar followed her, and the two engaged in conversation as they exited the rooftop.

Kareem's chest was tight. His hands fidgeted with anxiety. He squeezed his fists tight, waiting for his turn behind the others to go down the ladder. Why was Zara being so nice to Ashar? She almost never had anything that nice to say to Kareem...

Kareem? Binita's voice interrupted his thoughts. They were the only two left. Binita lowered onto the ladder up to her waist, holding the door open for Kareem to grab.

Sorry. He took over holding the door open, and waited for her to descend.

She didn't. *Maybe you might want to spend some time up here meditating,* she told him with a kind smile.

Kareem frowned. *Why?*

Something about our new teammate seems to be bothering you just a little.

I'm not bothered, Kareem said quickly.

Binita looked pointedly at his hands. He uncurled them, staring at the white marks in his palms. Perfect half-moons from where his nails had dug into his flesh.

You seem... a little... tense. Binita laughed. *It's just a thought.* Then she disappeared.

Kareem's frown deepened. He climbed down the ladder, closing the latch behind him, trying to shake off some of his anxiety. Of course he was tense. For obvious reasons. And none of them were the new teammate that had been thrust upon him.

Or the way Zara smiled at him when she talked.

CHAPTER 3

AURADAY DECEPTION

Auraday, the holiday where the Anunnaki celebrated their magical connection to the Aurastones, dawned bright and clear. Kareem yawned and stretched in his bed, listening to the bells as they welcomed the morning.

For just a second, homesickness swept through him.

Growing up, Auraday hadn't been as grand of a holiday at his home as it was here. In his home, he and his brother and sister received the traditional Auraday baskets, filled with small treats or a few items that they needed. They were a mix of human and Anunnaki items, and Kareem had always felt excited when he woke up on Auraday morning. He would try to beat Tejas and Akilah to the spot where the baskets lay, but somehow, Tejas would always manage to get there before him.

Those memories were warm, but there were new ones to be made here, at the House of the Venari. Sure, he'd still talk to his family before the day was done, but he was excited at the prospect of starting new memories and traditions. Ones that were his own. That granted him that adult feeling of independence.

I have them, Ovi called from the other side of the room.

Kareem threw his blankets off and sat up quickly. In front of Ovi sat the four decoy phones, their black screens gleaming in the dull lamplight.

Kareem's eyes flew between his friend and the phones. *Seriously, Ovi. How did you get these?*

I'd tell you, but I'd have to kill you, Ovi said with a wink.

Kareem laughed, partially because Ovi had amused him and partially in disbelief—they were finally getting somewhere with their plan! This was definitely different from waking up to his basket all the other Auraday mornings. But it was still an exciting and welcomed gift, nonetheless. Seeing Ovi laugh and joke again felt good.

Kareem picked up one of the devices and turned it over in his hand, checking it out before he looked back up and grinned at his roommate. *You're amazing. Seriously. I have no idea how you did it. I'm not sure I want to know, but you're amazing.*

I'll take that compliment. Ovi grinned back.

Kareem took a breath and stood. *Ready?*

Ready, Ovi responded.

They dressed, both wearing the traditional bright blue and white colors that marked the Auraday holiday. They concealed the phones in the pockets of their pants. The plan was to meet the girls in the Grand Hall and then use the distraction from the Auraday feast to get some of the research done. They weren't exactly supposed to have phones to begin with, so their time to use them would be limited. Taking advantage of the perfectly timed holiday distraction had been Binita's idea; as usual, Binita had displayed some of the quiet genius he was starting to expect from her. The dummy phones would be locked back in the adviser's office, and no one would be the wiser.

And they'd be one step closer to getting more information on SPE and finding Neelan.

Ovi and Kareem stepped outside into the sunny, bright morning. They hoped that by leaving the House early enough, the guard they were certain Savar had instructed to follow their every move wouldn't have time to learn their current whereabouts. Kareem glanced around the bustling city before them, craning his neck. *Have you seen Ashar?*

No. Ovi shook his head. *Not since training yesterday morning.*

Kareem frowned. Ashar had joined them on the rooftop every morning for the past week. He hadn't pressed any more about Auraday, which Kareem had been thankful for, but he had been continually interested in the group's powers. They had deflected many times. In fact, Zara had made a habit of deflecting by offering information about herself instead, which Ashar seemed to eat up. They walked to several of their classes together, and Kareem had to actively breathe to get through watching them without clenching his hands or his jaw. Binita's suggestion about meditating, while teasing, had actually served to be somewhat helpful in that situation.

Keep an eye out for him, Kareem said to Ovi as they walked in the direction of their planned meeting spot with the girls. *I wouldn't be surprised to find him following us.*

Ovi tilted his head. *You really don't like him, do you?*

No. Kareem shook his head. There was no point in hiding it from Ovi. His roommate was perceptive and smart, and Kareem hadn't exactly hidden his feelings well. *I don't.*

Why?

He hasn't earned it, Kareem responded honestly. He watched the corridor, his eyes searching for Binita and Zara. *The timing is just too suspicious. He just...* appears *a couple of weeks after we get back from Canada, right when we decide to go ahead and go after the phones? The process of getting to train here isn't as simple as it once was. Now, it's a heck of a lot more difficult than just being able to walk in. We know nothing about him, and he's suddenly placed on our team? Despite the fact that teams have been set and filled for months? It's too convenient,* Kareem said to Ovi.

Ovi nodded. *I get that. But what if it's just as weird of a situation for Ashar?*

Kareem's eyes narrowed. *Do you know something I don't know?*

No. Ovi's head shook. *I just get the sense that there's more to Ashar than meets the eye.*

Finally catching sight of Binita and Zara walking toward the Hall a little up ahead of them, Kareem grimaced.

I get the same impression, Ovi. I just plan for the worst.

And I tend to hope for the best, Ovi added sadly. Kareem sighed. Maybe Ovi was right. Ashar hadn't given Kareem any real reason to mistrust him.

But he hadn't offered reasons to trust him either.

Hey, Kareem said to the girls as they met in a heavily shaded and obscured spot behind a bunch of thick bushes and trees outside the Grand Hall.

Happy Auraday! Binita exclaimed. She put a set of blue beads over everyone's heads. Kareem ducked to receive his and then looked down.

What are these?

Fake Aurastones. Binita brimmed with excitement. *My family gives them out every year for Auraday.*

Don't you have to do something wild to get these? Zara asked as she examined her beads.

Binita smirked. *Only for people we don't like. We make them do dares. Otherwise, we give them to family and friends. Ya know... the people we care about.*

Sorry we don't have anything for you, Ovi said to her, looking grateful. *Thank you for mine, though.*

Binita's blush was a deeper red than the jewel-colored bow on her blue blouse. *Shall we?*

Kareem nodded. *Show us the way, Binita.*

They reemerged into the crowded square, filled with laughter and shouts and brightly colored outfits as people buzzed around them, participating in the day's festivities. The team trailed behind Binita, flitting in and out of groups of people as they made their way up the wide steps and inside the Grand Hall. They were practically unnoticed because so many others were coming and going as well.

Kareem was overwhelmed by being inside this place. Walking on the marble flooring. Staring at the incredible statues. Witnessing so many busy, important people scurrying by alone or in pairs, making hushed conversation, or looking over papers.

Somehow, Binita knew just how to navigate the massive structure's interior. They walked down a few cool hallways, and then Binita paused at the start of yet another corridor. *It's down this way,* she whispered.

Kareem peered down the hall. It was much more poorly lit than the others, with the majority of resources going to the fluttering decorations for Auraday that dangled from the ceiling. *Lead the way,* he gestured to Binita.

They slipped down the hall.

The cacophony of hurried footsteps and excited chattering slowly began to die out. Soon, only the sounds of their footsteps echoed off the stone floors. Finally, they reached the row of adviser's offices that—according to Binita—were typically locked during the day.

Binita stopped and pointed at one of the doors just up ahead. *That's it. We just need to...*

The door clicked.

It swung open.

And the group froze.

Kareem's heart slammed into his ribcage. They couldn't get caught. If they got caught, it was for sure over for them. Savar had made that crystal clear. They needed to hide. Kareem's eyes darted around the hallway. If they hid over behind that statue...

Footsteps drew his attention.

It was too late.

Adviser Eta, the queen's lead seer, stepped into the hall. Kareem had heard a lot about her, but he had never had a personal interaction with her. He was well aware that she would have become the Grand Elder had Queen Kinza never come along.

Kareem, Ovi, Binita, and Zara were in full view. They were maybe ten feet from the door, clearly coming toward it on a day when they shouldn't be there. In a place they shouldn't be. With phones they shouldn't have.

Kareem's brain wouldn't work. He tried to pull together some words that would help them. An excuse, a story, *anything*. He tried, but his mind swirled with confusion. He licked his dry lips, desperate to come up with anything that would keep his team safe.

Eta, however, didn't say anything to them. Her eyes were enormous in the dim light and luminous on her face. Her short hair and petite stature made her stand out in a crowd of busy Grand Hall workers. She looked at the group, her moonlike eyes glancing over all of them.

Then, she smiled.

Nodded.

Shut the door.

And walked down the hallway in the opposite direction.

For a long moment, Kareem and his team watched her go. When her shape finally disappeared at the opposite end of the hallway, he breathed out.

What was that? Zara's voice shook.

Kareem shook his head. *I have no idea. Do you think she's going to tell Savar?*

Do you think she locked the door? Binita added.

I don't know, Ovi said, plainly nervous. *Maybe we should...*

This seems like a boring way to spend Auraday, a familiar voice drawled.

Kareem spun so quickly that his head swam for a second. He aptly recovered and, in a flash, had his hand wrapped around Ashar's neck. *Where did you come from?* he snarled. He shoved Ashar back, slamming him against the stone wall of the hallway.

Ashar grunted but didn't fight back. *What do you mean, where did I come from? I'm not allowed to visit the Grand Hall?* he asked in a strained voice, Kareem's hand still tight around his neck until Zara came forward and pried the two boys apart.

Seriously, Kareem? she hissed.

Not when you're following us, Kareem said to Ashar, ignoring Zara.

Of course I'm following you. Aren't you my team? Aren't I supposed to stay with you? Train with you? Ashar's eyes grew hard. *You left me behind. I want to know why.*

We left you behind because this is none of your business, Kareem snapped. *Go back to the House. Enjoy the celebration. Just leave us alone.*

Ashar crossed his arms in defiance. *Not until you tell me what you're doing.*

Not a chance. Get out, Kareem said.

At the same time, Zara replied to Ashar with, *Do you promise not to tell anyone?*

Everyone looked at Zara with surprise.

What? Ashar stepped forward. Zara looked between him and Kareem, then settled her gaze on Ashar. *Do you promise not to tell anyone if we tell you what we're doing?*

Oh, yeah, *Zara. That's an* extremely *solid plan,* Kareem screeched. *There's no* way *that he could just lie and* say *that he won't tell anyone.* He grabbed Zara's shoulder, but she shrugged him off with a glare and turned back to Ashar.

Do you promise? she demanded again.

Ashar studied her. He looked back at Kareem, who was still seething with anger. *I promise.*

Good, Zara said.

Kareem was furious. *Zara, no!*

Zara pointed behind them. *We're breaking into that office to get some cell phones.*

Ashar's smile was bright and genuine. *Now* that's *an Auraday celebration.*

How could you do that?! Kareem exploded at Zara.

Ashar is right; he's our teammate, Kareem! she snapped back.

Kareem was aware that they were wasting time, but he was too angry to care. Zara had gone too far. She had betrayed not only Kareem but their whole group. She had made a decision he didn't approve of, but mostly, she had gone behind his back on something he had clearly expressed was important.

He wasn't about to let that slide.

Ashar smirked at all of them.

In the back of his mind, Kareem could hear Ovi and Binita as they started whispering to each other, paying the others no mind.

There's no way she didn't lock it, Ovi said.

I know, Binita agreed. *There's no way. So now we have to pick a lock.*

Can you pick locks?

Not that one, Binita said with a grimace. *I have lots of lockpicks, but that one has a magical seal that even I can't figure out.*

Most of Kareem's focus was still on Zara. He had made her so angry that he could practically see sparks flying from her hair. That was fine by him. He was just as mad.

I can't believe you, Kareem whisper-shouted at her. *You had no right.*

You're being an absolutely terrible leader, Zara hissed. *He deserves to know. He's not going anywhere, Kareem, and you need to just accept that! Besides, maybe he can help us to get into that office, which is the whole point of this plan, is it not?*

How could he possibly help to get through a locked door? Unless his power is teleportation or something, there's no way he can help us any better than we can help ourselves.

Ashar snorted. *How do you know my power isn't teleportation?*

I don't! Kareem threw his hands up in frustration. *That's the point! I don't know you. I don't know the first thing about you. I don't trust you, and I don't think that you're here to help us. I think you're here to report back to Savar what we're doing so that we get expelled.*

Zara arched an eyebrow at Kareem. *Well, now you've just given him even more information!*

Kareem's anger bubbled beneath his skin. *You appeared out of nowhere,* he growled at Ashar. *You followed us. If you want to prove yourself, do it now. Tell us what your ability is. Or give us a good enough reason to trust you, or I swear, I'll make your life absolutely miserable.*

Instead of responding, Ashar sauntered up to the door. He examined it, then he turned back, a wry smile on his lips. *Uh... the door's not even locked. Aren't we wasting time standing out here?* To the group's surprise, he reached out, grabbed the handle, and turned it. The door swung open on soundless hinges.

Kareem gaped. *She didn't lock it?* It made no sense. Adviser Eta had looked at them. How had she looked *directly* at them, closed the door, and left it unlocked?

She didn't lock the door, Ovi mumbled, echoing Kareem's shock.

Ashar grinned. *I'm good at getting into places I shouldn't. Abilities or not, it's just a talent I have. After you.* He gestured to Zara, who gave Kareem one last angry glance, then strode into the office.

Kareem followed, leaving Binita and Ovi to stand guard as planned.

Inside, the phones weren't hard to find. They were out on the desk in a pile, slapped together in a bin without any additional security. Kareem didn't hesitate. He reached forward and grabbed them, quickly swapping them out for the fake cell phones, and handed the real ones to the team.

They left swiftly, closing the door behind them with a soft click, and then they all hustled to the library. For the moment, Kareem was too high from the win of their plan working. For the moment, it didn't seem to bother him as much that Ashar was still tagging along with them.

THE ONGOING AURADAY celebration provided the perfect cover for the team to get some research done, locking themselves inside a study room at the library, where Kareem glanced at Zara, who still wouldn't look at him, and Ashar.

If you hear anything or anyone coming, you immediately tell us. Zara and I will try to help keep watch with you while we research, he said to Ashar, clearly implying that Ashar could not be trusted to watch the door on his own.

Ashar rolled his eyes. *I know how to pull guard duty.*

Again, why do you know that? Kareem narrowed his eyes. *Walking in off the street knowing how to be a lookout seems like a pretty specific skill set.*

Stop, Kareem, Zara sighed. *Seriously. Just shut up, watch the hall, and do some research. Leave him alone.*

Kareem snorted. He had no intention of leaving Ashar alone, but Zara was still mad at him. He wanted to offer her some kind of olive branch, so instead of doubling down on his position, he merely nodded.

Binita opened up one of the phones. *Three hours. That's how long until the final toasts. Let's make the most of it,* she said and nodded at the others.

With notepads and pens out on the table, Kareem, Zara, and

Ovi opened up the other three phones and began to type. Thanks to Binita, they had a play-by-play agenda for the celebration. They knew exactly who was going to give a toast, which instructor would insist on playing an Auraday game, and most importantly, how long each of those events would take. They had several hours of uninterrupted time in front of them, and Kareem was determined to make the most of it. They poured over the four cell phones, furiously typing and swiping and occasionally writing down a note or grunting in frustration as the phones' batteries crept toward zero.

While they worked, Kareem repeatedly shot Ashar dirty looks, not caring if Ashar noticed them or not. And even if he did notice it, Ashar seemed to pretend Kareem wasn't glaring at him, keeping his eyes trained on the door, occasionally poking his head out to make sure no one was approaching their room.

The first hour went by quickly. No one talked. Every now and then, Kareem heard a wave of cheers from the celebrations outside the library's walls. Ashar kept watch, and the other four kept their heads bent, trying to find dirt on SPE. Zara and Kareem lifted their heads occasionally to make sure Ashar was still doing his job.

It was in the second hour that Kareem, feeling like he was getting nowhere with his research, began to let his mind wander. He knew the others wanted him to include Ashar in the team. Zara was right: having Ashar there had been an asset. Who knew how long it would have taken them to simply just try the door and see if it was open if Ashar hadn't done it?

Still, he didn't trust him. He didn't *want* to trust him, either. In actuality, Kareem would have preferred Ashar had *nothing* to do with their mission. He didn't want to go into detail with the newbie about Neelan and the ubir in Canada. At least, to his credit, Ashar hadn't asked any more questions. He'd been a perfect lookout, quiet and attentive.

Kareem was about to say something, albeit begrudgingly,

about his appreciativeness of Ashar keeping watch and keeping silent, when he saw Ashar's eyes wander back to Zara.

So, Ashar asked her, his tone casual, *is this your favorite Auraday ever or what?*

Zara smiled at him, an action that made Kareem's stomach clench. *It's up there,* she told him. Kareem detected a heavy sarcasm in her tone. She was being playful with Ashar.

Kareem hated it. He looked over at Binita and Ovi, and they all exchanged weirded-out expressions while Zara and Ashar continued to chat.

Oh yeah? Ashar raised an eyebrow at her. *One of your top ten?*

I don't think I have a top ten. Top three, maybe. And this one might just make the cut. I haven't decided, Zara replied, winking at him. Kareem tried to suppress a growl.

Ashar grinned back at her. *I've definitely never experienced one this exciting. That's for sure.*

If you want to call it that, Zara shrugged. *It's not the word I'd use to describe what we're doing in here. But it's... different. A good different, I think.*

Due to the events or due to the company? Ashar's smirk was so self-satisfied Kareem had to physically resist the urge to smack it off his face. Zara giggled, and suddenly, Kareem was so intensely angry he had to breathe out through his nose.

Instead of waiting to hear Zara's response, he looked up sharply at Binita and Ovi. *What are you guys finding so far?*

Binita sighed and shook her head. *Nothing, really. Pretty much only what we already know. SPE appears to be a research organization. Doing good deeds, following up with important medical discoveries...* She looked thoroughly disappointed in herself, dropping her chin in her palm with a pout at her phone screen.

Yeah, Ovi agreed. *Their website is very flashy but without much substance. Great graphics, little content.*

Kareem grimaced, glancing at his phone, which was also open

to the website. Smiling, bland faces, glossy and human, filled the screen. *That can't be it.*

I know, Binita agreed. *It's obviously a front. I just can't seem to get underneath it to find what the front is for.*

We can do this, Kareem tried. *We have to get to the bottom of this. If anyone can figure it out, it's probably you two.*

Next to them, Zara was still turned in her chair—all the way around—to flirt with Ashar, neither of them listening to their conversation. Ovi shook his head. *Your faith in me is both overwhelming and misplaced. Whoever SPE is and whatever they do, they know how to cover their tracks.*

Let's keep digging, Kareem urged. *There's got to be something.*

Both Ovi and Binita nodded but didn't respond, so Kareem sighed and turned to Zara.

He nearly shouted in frustration—Ashar had somehow sidled closer to Zara. He had her hand in his, palm facing up, and was tracing one of the lines across her palm. The movement was far too slow and far too full of contact for Kareem's comfort.

He moved and pulled Zara's hand back. *That's not standing guard,* he snapped at Ashar.

Oh please, Ashar scoffed. *It's not like anyone is coming. They're all getting drunk and congratulating themselves on a job well done.*

You appeared out of nowhere, Kareem hissed. *What's to keep someone else from doing that?*

I'd know if someone was there.

Not if you're too busy flirting to pay attention! Kareem snapped right back.

Kareem! Zara sneered at him. *He wasn't flirting with me!*

Oh, he most definitely was. Why else was he touching your hand like that?

He was reading my palm, Zara snapped.

That's not even real. Or useful, Kareem said, his gaze bouncing between the two of them.

Ashar's expression sharpened. *It's more useful than this stupid guard duty you're having me do. I could help, you know.* He gestured to one of the phones. *Just tell me what you're looking for. I promise you, I can find it.*

No way. Absolutely not. Kareem laughed.

Ashar merely smirked at him before turning his attention back to Zara. *Zara, what do you think? Do* you *want my help?*

Zara looked at Kareem. *We need all the help we can get. Maybe he could... be... useful.*

I will never... Kareem began, but emotion cut off his words. He gulped, trying to find them around the swirl of feelings in his mind. *I—*

I found something, Ovi's voice cut him off. *Guys. Check this out.*

Kareem, Zara, and Binita crowded around Ovi and his phone, and when Ashar made a move to join them, Kareem tried to shoulder him away.

He's part of it now, Zara chided. *Just let him stay. I'm going to fill him in on everything later, anyway.*

Kareem would rather have swallowed a jar full of udadiy—bee-like insects with painful stingers native to Rhapta—but glancing at the clock, he nodded. There was only an hour left of the celebration outside, so he couldn't waste time by arguing.

What is it? Kareem prompted Ovi.

Ovi held up one of the phones. *It's a stretch. One of the researchers named in this article about cancer research has ties to SPE.*

How does that help? Zara asked.

Ovi grinned. *I found his address. Northern California.*

Kareem blinked. That was a long way from Rhapta. Especially when they were banned from leaving.

Okay, he said, looking at the group. *It's small but good. It's better than nothing. Thanks, Ovi.*

Ovi nodded.

Binita clicked her phone off. *I think that's all we're going to find tonight. I don't know what else to try looking up.*

Kareem sighed. *Same here. I'm out of other ideas. For now, let's go back to the celebration. Everyone is drunk enough now they won't even notice we've been missing. Enjoy. Have fun. We'll circle back on the rooftop tomorrow.*

They all nodded, and together, they moved to leave the study room, Binita and Ovi exiting first. Ashar stepped toward the door but lingered. Kareem looked at Zara, who pointedly looked away.

He stepped toward her. *Zara, I—*

Come on, Ashar, Zara said, cutting Kareem off and grabbing Ashar's hand. *Let's see if this will become my favorite Auraday ever.*

Ashar didn't say anything, but the look he shot Kareem was nothing short of triumphant. Kareem watched them walk, hand-in-hand, down the hall.

He breathed deeply, telling himself not to think about them anymore. He had to focus on what was more important. Finding Neelan, learning about SPE—those were his priorities right now. He didn't care what Zara and Ashar did.

He nodded to himself, straightened up, and left the study room. At least now they had a lead. Somewhere to start looking. Sure, what Ovi found wasn't much, but it was better than nothing. And, as he left the library and joined the festivities outside, he clung to that belief.

It was the only thing that kept him from feeling like the day was very much a loss.

CHAPTER 4

A TEST OF LOYALTY

Auraday's remnants littered the halls of the House of the Venari the next morning. As Kareem and Ovi picked their way through them, driven from their room by their lingering excitement over their success of the previous night, they avoided the listless banners draped over random surfaces and the confetti crumbling to dust along the ground. Around them, their classmates and teachers staggered down the hallways with tired eyes and green faces—the after-effects from the previous day's festivities. When Kareem and Ovi arrived in the dining hall, Kareem noted how it could easily have been confused for a crime scene. Glitter winked from random corners, streamers lay broken and ripped over the tables, and trash and dirty dishes piled up on the tables. Moving swiftly and quietly around them, workers were scrambling to get the place back in tip-top shape.

Kareem and Ovi grabbed their spicy teas and breakfast and sat at a table that had just been cleaned. *Must have been some party,* Ovi observed as they watched a surprisingly still-hungover—given their fast healing abilities—adult hastily mop up the tea that over-flowed from his cup while his eyes had been shut. He grunted, trying to stem the tide of bitter liquid that collected beneath the dispenser.

I guess, Kareem agreed, surprised to see his teachers as bent out of shape as they were. Had they even *tried* to be responsible last night so they could resume their professional demeanors in front of their student in the morning?

But then he found his eyes sliding to where Zara and Binita were entering the hall, followed by Ashar, who flashed a devilish smile Kareem's way as he prowled after the girls. Kareem breathed in harshly; it was never a welcome sight, Ashar tagging along with the others in the group. He told himself it wasn't just Zara. It was seeing Ashar hanging around *any* of them.

Ovi snorted. *Let it go, man.* He prodded Kareem with one sharp finger. *He's not that bad.*

He's so pompous, Kareem snarled. His eyes remained glued to them. Ashar caught up with Zara and Binita and slung his long, muscular arms around both of their shoulders. Zara laughed, a sound that was loud and almost unwelcome in the quiet morning in the hall. Kareem resisted the urge to growl. *Look at him. At the way he acts. He thinks he's a king or something.*

So what? You gotta let it go, Kareem.

Kareem rolled his eyes at his friend. Ovi rolled his right back.

Seriously. He kept our secret last night. He could have run straight to Savar, but he didn't. He's great at combat, he's smart, and Zara is in an uncharacteristically good mood when he's around. I mean this in the nicest way possible: I think you should back off a little. Maybe work instead on what it would take for you to give him a chance.

Kareem grunted in response and made a deliberate effort to keep Ashar out of his field of view as he turned his head. He hated that he let Ashar get under his skin so easily. He wished he could— and knew he should—take Ovi's advice. But one look at their new teammate, and Kareem's blood began to instantly boil. Maybe the others didn't see or feel what he felt, but something in his gut told him something wasn't right about Ashar. Logically, Ovi was right in that Ashar hadn't run to Savar after the previous night's phone raid, and he had been doing the best he could to get up to speed with the rest of the team. He was useful, he was smart, and Kareem knew that, all things considered, Ashar wasn't a terrible teammate to have.

He had a choice to make. Either accept Ashar and bring him up to speed or figure out a way to prove that his instincts were right and that Ashar was hiding something.

Moments later, the source of his ire, along with Binita and Zara, joined them at the table.

Morning, Kareem directed at the trio. He was, if he did say so himself, remarkably calm when greeting Ashar. Zara's eyes widened marginally, and Binita tilted her head when she looked at him, but both nodded.

Morning, they chorused.

Looks like we missed out on something good, Ashar smirked. He waited until Binita and Zara sat, then pulled a chair in between them. He stretched his arms upward, then dramatically dropped one down to circle the back of Zara's chair. Why did it look like he was staking some sort of claim over her? And why did it bother Kareem so much? Was it maybe because it had taken quite a bit of time and effort before Zara finally talked to him and saw him as something a little more than dirt underneath her fingernail, yet she accepted Ashar's friendship and flirtations without even batting an eyelash?

Kareem swallowed. *Auraday must've gotten a little out of control,* he responded casually.

Zara raised an eyebrow as she looked around the messy hall. *That's what I was thinking. I know this is our first time experiencing it while living here, but I wonder... Is it always like this?*

I'll have to ask Tejas, Kareem responded. Tejas had never mentioned anything about Auraday here with the Venari before, nor had Kareem ever heard of the celebration at the House of the Venari being a little bigger than any home-oriented one. Indeed, it did seem that this Auraday had somehow had some kind of extra significance given to it by the school. Auraday was always celebratory, sure, but the celebration at the House seemed to have been above and beyond. After they had left the library last night, they all stayed out in the square and enjoyed the festivities for a bit, and then when Kareem and Ovi made their way back to the House to head to bed, they had been astonished to see that the party had made its way inside the House. Not all that long ago, Venari used to be avoided at all costs.

Things really had changed in Rhapta.

Who? Ashar asked him.

His brother, Zara answered, giving Kareem a shrug. *He's a Venari.*

Kareem returned his gaze to his tea. He wondered how much Ashar knew about him. About all of them. If he'd been getting intel from Zara directly, or of he'd been doing his own research, was it possible he already knew that Tejas was Kareem's brother and only pretended not to? Ovi wanted him to accept Ashar and lay off, but there was just something about Ashar's whole persona that felt like a well-crafted performance, glossy and shiny, something that held just enough surface tension that any suspicion would slide right off for most people. He seemed calculated. Not real. Like at all times, thoughts were swirling around in his brain about things no one else knew or understood. An ulterior motive.

Ashar leaned toward Zara and whispered something in her ear, earning another quiet laugh from her.

At the very least, Kareem needed to understand why it bothered him so much to see Zara's reaction to the new recruit.

The group then sat in silence, joining in the muted atmosphere of the dining hall until Binita's chair squeaked as she scooted it back, the sound cutting loudly through the air.

Kareem and the others looked up as Binita blinked, standing with her tea in hand. *Um, I...I'm going to take off,* she declared. Kareem frowned as he watched her walk away.

Where is she going? he asked Zara, thinking she'd know best since they were roommates.

How should I know, Kareem? she huffed in exasperation. *I'm not her mother.*

No one ever knows with her, Ovi added.

Kareem was curious. Binita had gotten up so abruptly. She looked almost nervous.

Well, is she okay? Kareem asked.

Seems to me like she likes being by herself, Ashar commented.

Because you *know her so well,* Kareem muttered.

She does *like to be alone sometimes, actually,* Zara replied to Ashar while glaring at Kareem. *That's absolutely a correct assumption, Ashar. Ignore Kareem. I do.*

Kareem made a chuffing noise.

I'll check on her later, Ovi said. *I'm sure it's nothing, Just Binita being Binita.*

Yeah, Kareem nodded at him. *Maybe check, just in case.*

Mental Conditioning class, which had long been Kareem's least favorite course, proved to be incredibly challenging once again, but only because his mind constantly wandered down the many paths it would rather be taking than being present in that classroom. He wasn't good at it, and the instructor, Laban Dayal, hated his guts. Kareem knew it was important to pay attention, especially if he wanted to graduate in record time like he told himself he wanted to do before he even stared training, but it was nearly impossible to focus as Laban droned on about mindful walking and focus anchors, repeatedly referencing his top student and how well she was doing in the class—Binita. Binita was great at mental conditioning. She had been trying to help Kareem get better at it, too.

But Kareem was bored. And, being bored, his mind decided to chew on subjects that were far more delicious than the memory palace technique or the dangers of fatigue.

As Binita was called on—yet again—Kareem eyed her. Where had she gone that morning? Why had she left so abruptly? Currently, she was sitting in front of him in class, being Laban's favorite student as usual. She greeted him when they sat down, but she hadn't mentioned anything about why she had to leave breakfast.

In addition, he couldn't keep his eyes off where Ashar and Zara sat three rows in front of him.

You're going to burn a hole in them if you stare any harder, Ovi whispered. Kareem flinched at Ovi's fingers as they flicked the back of his wrist.

Ouch, he muttered.

Tell me you didn't need a reminder to come back to reality, Ovi said quietly.

Kareem's breath hissed out of his nostrils, and he sucked another back in. *No. But does he have to sit so close?* He continued to watch closely, Laban's words washing over him unheard.

Ovi merely shook his head and went back to paying attention.

The minutes stretched. When Kareem noticed Ashar flinch, his suspicion roused. Had Ashar moved so suddenly at something Laban just said? Was he in pain from something? Had Kareem imagined it? He narrowed his eyes, studying the long plane of Ashar's shoulders.

Movement jolted him out of his scrutiny. The class was standing, and Kareem craned his neck to look around the room before he joined them.

What's happening? he asked Ovi.

Partner work. Analyzing chapters sixteen through thirty, Ovi replied.

Partners? His head went to Zara. Who would she pair up with?

Ovi snorted. *Ya know, you might actually stand a chance if you run over there right now.*

A small circle of other girls had formed around Ashar. Between the coy glances and simpering words, it was pretty easy to tell what was going on. And Ashar appeared to be gloating as he basked in the sea of feminine attention. He wore a stupid smile on his face as he soaked it up, almost as though he had temporarily forgotten all about Zara and her existence.

Please, Laban's dreary, deep, telepathic voice cut through the din. *Choose your partner wisely, and return once you've completed your analysis of strategies for peak performance and how to unleash your mental fortitude.*

Kareem approached Zara, lightly tapping her on the shoulder. *Partners?*

Zara shrugged, eyeing the crowd around Ashar. *Why not?*

Kareem's chest expanded, but he inhaled to quickly diminish the hope bubbling up. Zara seemed to be in a good mood. He was afraid to do or say anything to ruin it. Instead, he simply smiled and followed her to the edge of the classroom, where they sat at one of the worn tables and pulled out their books. He cast a glance back at Ashar. *Sorry to be your second choice,* he blurted.

Zara's eyebrows rose. *What makes you think that?*

Kareem blinked. *I... um... You didn't want to work with Ashar?*

It's not like I was about to fight for it, she said with a toss of her long hair over her shoulder. *If he wanted to work with me, he would have asked.*

Kareem picked a spot on the table where the wood had been hit with something hard enough to splinter it. He pulled a few flecks away before looking at Zara. *He really likes the attention, huh?*

She rolled her eyes. *Kareem, just drop it, will you? I'm so sick of hearing you grumbling about him. Ashar is fun to be around. He's not the monster you, for some reason, think he is. Stop being so... annoying, okay?*

Kareem gestured to the continual crowd of fluttering eyelashes and overly bright laughter. *How come he seems more than willing to tell* them *all about himself, but he won't tell us anything? I'm telling you, Zara, he—*

Oh please. *He's not telling them anything,* Zara responded primly, rifling through her book as she searched for the correct chapter. *Those girls only* think *they know about him. But Ashar's told me it's all just rumors.*

Kareem frowned. *What do you mean?*

Seriously, Kareem. Where have you been?

What are they saying about him? he pressed, ignoring her jab. Rumors had to start somewhere, didn't they? Perhaps, he thought, this was the way he would finally determine what was bothering him so much about Ashar. Surely, there had to be some truth to the rumors, wild though they might be as they flew around Ashar's presence.

They're saying that he's been on the run for years, Zara said as she watched Ashar. *He grew up in a crime family. He knows how to evade the government, live off the grid.*

Like, outside of Rhapta?

She shrugged. *I don't know. I guess.*

He let out a fake laugh. *What a bunch of lies.*

There's another rumor that he's a hitman. That one is probably a little far-fetched.

Seems more likely to me, Kareem muttered under his breath. If Zara had heard it, she didn't act like it.

You should try talking to him, Kareem, Zara suggested, *without being a complete mpumbavu about it. Figure out the truth for yourself. Maybe he'd want to tell you a little more about himself if you weren't so rude and distrusting all the time.*

I shouldn't have to pry basic information out of him, Kareem snapped. *If he's so normal, why can't he just explain who he is and why he's suddenly here? And what his ability is?*

Ovi and Binita paired up, and they drifted over, settling in across from them.

Maybe he's nervous around you, Binita added softly, as though she had been there all along. *Maybe he doesn't feel comfortable telling you about himself when you seem to hate him so much.*

Ha! Kareem chided. *Him. Nervous. Come on, Binita.* He opened his book and followed where Zara pointed, his mind perplexed as the words swam on the page in front of him. He was so preoccupied that he missed Ashar's presence until he spoke to them.

Well, if it isn't my team, team-ing without me.

What, your crowd of simpering followers wasn't enough? Kareem snapped automatically. *You've got lots of partners to pick from over there.*

Ashar's smirk grew. *Simpering?* It was like the mere thought of it delighted him. Kareem could see his ego inflating. It was irritating to watch. How was he supposed to be nice to someone like him?

I'd say so, Zara said, her voice sharp as a sword.

Like you didn't notice, Kareem seethed. *You were just standing over there, basking as they fussed over you.*

Fussed over me? Ashar threw his head back and laughed. *I'm sorry, Kareem. I can't help it if I get more female attention than you. You sound jealous.*

You insolent... Kareem started, his nails digging into the palms of his hands underneath the table.

What? Ashar dared, jutting his chin out. His shoulders tightened, and Kareem recognized as he settled into a fighting stance. *What do you want to say to me now? Huh, Kareem?*

Zara and Binita protested, but Kareem was deaf to them. Blood rushed through his ears, and he tensed. He was about to call Ashar a slew of names, but then a figure standing in the hall outside the cracked-open door stopped him before he could do so.

It was Tejas. His brother was raising his eyebrows at Kareem, beckoning him to sneak out into the hall so they could talk.

"Uh, I have to use the bathroom!" Kareem called to the teacher, his hand shooting up. The class turned as one, looking at him. Laban briefly glared at him and then made a shooing motion with his hand before returning to help one of the groups.

Kareem jumped up and stormed out of the room, following his brother into the hall. He felt the eyes of his team on him as he left, but he tried to brush it off as he moved forward.

What? he snapped at Tejas, sounding rude even though he hadn't meant to.

Tejas's eyebrows pinched with amusement. *What's with you?*

Nothing. Kareem didn't look at him as they strolled down the hallway, away from the classroom.

Tejas shot him an encouraging smile. *Well... how's it going?*

Fine. They stopped walking. *Tejas, did you need something?*

I really am checking in on you, Kareem. You're not exactly sailing smoothly through the year.

How did you know? Kareem asked with heavy sarcasm in his tone. Then he stood straighter. *Everything's good now. I haven't gotten into any more trouble. Did Mom put you up to this?*

Tejas's eyebrows rose again. *No, she didn't. Kareem—you got back from near death in Canada, and you want to tell me that every-thing is fine? No struggles, no nothing?*

Kareem blew out a breath and looked up and down the hall. This *is where you want to have this conversation?*

When they first returned from Canada and their fight with the ubir, Tejas had given him a very stern dressing down around what had transpired. Kareem wished Tejas had heard the story from him first instead of Savar, but he couldn't change the past. Kareem did think it would have been nice, in retrospect, to have his big brother on his team, then *and* now.

Tejas grabbed Kareem, and Kareem squirmed against the brotherly headlock.

Let me go!

Tejas laughed. *Come on.* He released Kareem. *Let's talk somewhere else, then.*

They walked outside to the gardens. In the moist Rhapta air, ferns of various sizes unfurled their blades of leaves as they absorbed the winter sunshine. Butterflies fluttered around blossoms of colorful flowers. The gardens were still kept clean and neat for any students who might be interested in becoming herbalists, and Kareem and Tejas wandered the path of gray crushed stone through well-kept beds. The weather was so nice out that with every step, he felt some of his anger dissipate until, finally, he was as calm as the plants around them.

So—doesn't seem like you like the new kid much, Tejas said, finally breaking the silence.

Kareem sighed. *Is it that obvious?*

Oh yes, extremely so. Abundantly, I might say, Tejas teased. *So much so that even I've heard of your ongoing feud with him.*

How? Kareem's brother was twelve years older than him. He had gone on over fifty assignments. He was a busy guy.

Ashar apparently has some kind of air of mystery about him, Tejas observed, *and everyone seems to love it. Girls, guys, and everyone in between. Stands to reason the one person who doesn't like him is a little bit of a cause for some intense gossip himself.* He smiled, but his eyes were pinched with worry at the corners, and Kareem looked away.

I just don't trust him, Kareem said with a sullen kick at a rock. *He appeared out of nowhere. I thought the House never got new students mid-term. He just... appeared and joined my team. My team, of all teams. There's too much unknown, and it all centers around him.*

I know, Tejas agreed. *Hence, man of mystery.*

Mysteries can be dangerous, Kareem muttered.

Tejas laughed. *You've always been wary of the unknown, little brother. That's okay.* He stopped and laid a hand on Kareem's shoulder. *Wariness is good, especially after all you've been through.*

Kareem shook off the hand. *I know. So why does my team act like I'm the crazy one?*

You're not, Tejas responded. *But even with that... are you all right?*

Kareem sighed. Tejas couldn't be trusted with what Kareem and his team were dedicated to with SPE and Neelan. He chewed on the moment, unwilling to lie to his brother but knowing that if Tejas knew everything, he would try to stop Kareem and his friends.

I'm fine, he settled on. *Things are fine.*

Well, as far as lies go, that might be your worst. Talk to me, Kareem. You were so excited to start training. You're not acting like yourself.

He looked at his brother. *Really. Everything is fine. We're just... focused on keeping out of trouble.*

Tejas's eyes searched his face. He did his best to keep his expression, but his heart beat rapidly as he waited for Tejas to say something. Part of him wanted Tejas to call him out. To offer assistance. To swoop in and take over, to make everything better. A bigger part, however, recognized that Tejas didn't understand. He knew his brother would always support him and would always strive to do what was right. In Tejas's mind, however, the missing Anunnaki were not a problem that should be solved by Venari in training. Kareem knew Tejas would take the information straight to Savar. That, ultimately, was not acceptable. So far, Savar had done nothing with the information he already had.

Finally, Tejas smiled. *Well. I'm glad you're keeping out of trouble, at least. One less thing I have to worry about.*

Kareem raised an eyebrow. *You, the star of Savar's skies, worry? What could the model Venari student worry about other than keeping his nose firmly planted in the administration's business?*

Tejas gave him a playful shove. *Watch it. One of us has to uphold the family name.*

Glad that's you, Kareem responded. He meant it. Tejas was his brother, and while he loved his brother with all his heart, it was becoming more and more apparent to Kareem they were very different people. Being here and training to be Venari might mean they had another thing in common, but it didn't mean the same thing.

Kareem would not let the disappearance of the Anunnaki stand. Tejas was content to hand it over to Savar and say his part was done.

Come on, Tejas gestured back to the main building. *Let's get you back before Ashar steals all of your spotlight.*

I'm not jealous of that, Kareem insisted.

Sure, little brother. Sure, Tejas responded with a wry grin.

Kareem sighed and followed his brother back to class. He knew Tejas was letting something slide from their conversation. He just wasn't quite sure which part.

CHAPTER 5
HIDDEN TRUTHS

Ovi had followed Binita before, so shadowing her steps down the dark hallway didn't feel nearly as invasive as it should. Still, it felt wrong as he walked after her into the quiet of the abandoned wing of the school.

Ovi told himself he had justification. He had promised Kareem he would check on her and make sure she was okay. And by following her, he was following through on that promise, right?

Besides, he also wanted to keep Binita safe from harm. Though she often disappeared on her own, the recent danger hung over all of their heads, and Ovi didn't like the thought of Binita being alone. She could be taken. Or she could be doing something that would ultimately lead to her demise. Or maybe she wasn't *mentally* okay. She herself could be hurting, hiding her pain over the traumatic experience in Canada in ways Ovi was achingly familiar with. He didn't want her to suffer alone like he did. If she was in pain, he wanted to know. Even more than he wanted to fulfill the word he had given to Kareem.

In typical Binita fashion, she seemed to float aimlessly. She meandered over stone floors and around wooden doors, picking her way through on a path only she seemed to know. Here and there, she stopped, her focus catching on random details Ovi would have otherwise missed. A stone fresco, a lock, a crumble of trash heaped into a corner.

Ovi frowned, examining each piece of evidence after she moved on, searching for something that would indicate her intentions. He found nothing. Her movements felt random. She would take three fast steps, then slow down for one. She would stop to make note of the details in a carving but ignore entirely another statue as it leered at her from the sides of the building. No, Ovi surmised, Binita had almost no method to her madness.

Until, of course, she disappeared.

Ovi froze.

He had followed her into a long-forgotten hallway deep in the science section of the training grounds. Here, classrooms were often closed off because of some magical mishap or another, and they had been warned initially to treat such a section with care. Among students, it was said this was the most haunted area in the whole school, as it contained the souls of students who had long since succumbed to either the magical disaster that had turned the lab into an off-limits section or had died of curiosity years after.

Ovi didn't believe in ghosts.

However, when a hand snaked out of the darkness of an empty classroom, his heart startled, and his mind supplied the least logical explanation possible. He tripped, pulled into the darkness by the hand. He stumbled, then righted himself, preparing for a fight.

Who's there? he called.

I think you know—you're the one who's been following me and all, Binita's cool voice said. Ovi relaxed. The room was dark, but as his eyes adjusted, he could see Binita had created a small nook in the otherwise empty room, sectioned off by desks piled on top of each other. He watched as Bonita crawled through an opening of the desk mountain and decided to go in after her. Inside the fort, the ceiling of it created by old, tattered blankets tied to chair legs on one side and pinned to the wall on the other, she twisted the dial on a small, portable lantern, and light flooded the darkness, and Ovi blinked again.

What is this place?

Binita grabbed an old leather floor cushion, gesturing for Ovi to sit in it, and he gingerly lowered himself into the flaking seat. She then dragged one of the old desks with its chair attached over to him and sat in it. *Didn't you ever make forts as a child?*

Ovi gaped at her. Clearly, Binita didn't know him well at all. His childhood had not exactly been conducive to the whimsy of fort-making. *No,* he offered simply.

Binita's smile was wry. *I did. But not for fun. I learned how to create spaces where I could be safe. Where I could hide if I needed to.*

Ovi leaned forward. *From who?*

Anyone. Everyone. The ability to be unnoticed is important to me.

Ovi nodded. He didn't press. *I understand that,* he said quietly.

Binita cast him a glance. *I see.*

I don't think you do, but maybe we can get there. Ovi leaned back. He nodded to the piled desks. *This is quite a fort.*

Thank you, Binita responded.

Why did you make it?

Fidgeting, Binita picked at a particularly rough spot on the cushion. *I guess... I don't know. I'm still shaken up by what happened with the ubir.*

Ovi frowned. *We're safe here,* he assured her. *Nothing is going to come to us here. Not while Savar is here and all of the other Venari.*

I know that, Binita said quietly. *Or...*

Ovi waited patiently.

Binita blew out a breath. *I thought I knew that. But I'm afraid, Ovi. I... I think I'm very afraid.*

Ovi did smile then. *I am, too.*

You are? she asked sharply.

Ovi nodded and rose from his seat. He wandered, hunched over because of the low blanket-ceiling, to where Binita sat, wondering briefly what it would be like to touch her, even the fabric of her clothing. Instead, he set his hand atop the desk, close to hers but not touching. Never touching.

I am.

Binita stared at their hands, and Ovi's eyes followed. It was silent for a beat before he pulled away and stood straight.

So, I-I guess I understand what you're going through, he clarified, his face slightly heating up. He thought back to that day. How could he tell Binita that he was scared by the ubir, but he had been even more terrified of himself?

Kareem and Zara act so unaffected, she said. *I almost think they're totally fine.*

Maybe they're just good actors.

Maybe.

So. He sighed, wanting to change the subject because he could sense that Binita was feeling uncomfortable. *Why have you been coming here?*

She shrugged. *Mostly, I just need the time. I don't want to be constantly tuned in to the Kareem-Zara-Ashar show. And,* she added, *I need the time to think.*

Ovi nodded. *They're ridiculous sometimes, aren't they?*

A little bit. Maybe, Binita said. Then she shot him a wry smile. *Okay, yeah—they totally are.*

They make it difficult to keep the group focused on what we've been trying to do.

Right? Binita's smile crept across her face in a slow bloom. *Honestly, I need to spend more time thinking about that article and what we know about SPE and less time watching Kareem struggle with his big feelings and Zara trying to light them on fire.*

Ovi laughed. *And Ashar dancing around them.*

Definitely, Binita agreed. *So, yeah. I've been coming here to think, to feel safe. Just to exist, really.*

Ovi glanced around. *Have you been doing much thinking about the information we found the other day?*

Yes, actually. Her chest puffed up with pride. *And I think that… well, I think I might have something.*

What? What is it? Ovi felt the swoop of hope in his chest.

Binita grinned. *Let me show you something.*

She rose and quickly trotted into a corner of the room. She rustled around, and Ovi stared curiously at her. Strange noises and clicks emanated from that side of the room, and Ovi's concern grew. He was just about to stand and offer to help when Binita made a small exclamation of excitement. *What's happening over there?* he called.

One moment, Binita replied. Patiently, Ovi waited, his hands folded tightly against himself. What was she up to this time?

Finally, a bluish-green glow lit up the corner of the room, and Binita beamed in the light.

A computer! Ovi stood, his steps fast as he traveled, and quickly joined her. Together, they watched the screen come to life. *Where did you find this?* Computers weren't unheard of in Rhapta. The internet was accessible to many private citizens. However, the Venari limited access for students as a precaution. So, finding a computer here was a little bit of a windfall.

Stashed in this wing, Binita clarified. *Clearly, nobody knows what they have in here.*

Clearly, Ovi agreed. It was such a treasure that surely, if anyone knew of its existence, they would hoard it as closely as Binita had. He looked back at the screen. *What have you been doing on it?*

I was doing a little research on my own even before we found the phones on Auraday, Binita said shyly. She tapped on some keys, and the computer screen slowly brought up a document. *I think that I have found another connection.*

A sound caught both of their attention. It was a sharp crack, different enough from the normal groans and creaks of the abandoned wing.

Ovi's heart rate rose. He looked at Binita. *Any idea what that was?*

She shook her head, and his heart clenched as her face whitened. *No,* she said in a small voice. *I—you don't think...*

It's nothing serious, I'm sure, Ovi reassured her with a confidence he didn't feel. *Probably just a mouse or something. A bird tapping at the window.*

As if on cue, the sound occurred again. This time, Ovi recognized that it easily could be the random scratches of an animal that had somehow found its way into the building. That, he reasoned, was the most logical explanation. However, his fear mirrored the look on Binita's face. *Uh, maybe we should go on and head back to the others,* he suggested. *Whatever it is will be gone eventually.*

Binita looked around with wide, shifty eyes as she nibbled on her bottom lip. *Yeah. Good thinking. Maybe meet me back here tomorrow before we meet with the others on the roof?* The gang had plans to meet before combat training, which was already super early in the morning.

But Ovi thought it would be worth it to meet up with her again.

Only if you want me to, he said. *I know this is your safe place. I shouldn't have been following you. I was just worried. You know. About you being alone after...*

She stared at him, not saying a word. It made Ovi nervous.

If you don't want me to come back, I won't, he babbled, wanting to fill the silence.

When she finally smiled, warmth filled him, and he was able to relax. *You can come back anytime,* she told him. *I—it's nice that you know about it, actually.*

Ovi beamed. He liked that now the both of them had a shared

secret. A shared place. He quickly realized he liked the idea of coming back. It felt special. Binita had been vulnerable with him, and it made him feel like maybe he could be a bit more open around her. He seemed to relate to her more than the others in the group, and he sort of thought Binita felt the same way. And, if Binita could share her secret with him, perhaps he could do the same.

He tilted his head as something else occurred to him. *Should we invite the others?*

Binita hesitated. *I... Um...*

I know what you mean, Ovi laughed.

She huffed. *It's not that I don't want them to be here or to see it. It's just that everyone is so... tense.*

Hey, I get it. You don't need them coming here and acting out like they do everywhere else.

Yeah. I don't want the drama.

No drama, he agreed.

They shut the computer down and then walked out into the hall. When they came back to the main promenade, Binita paused. She turned to Ovi, and he froze as her eyes met his.

Thank you, she said sincerely. *I hadn't realized how much I needed someone else to know how I was feeling. I appreciate it, Ovi.* She smiled, and he smiled back.

Of course. Anytime.

Binita nodded, bit her bottom lip again, and then walked away. As Ovi watched her, his chest felt a sort of fluttering feeling. He wasn't quite sure what to make of it. But maybe Binita could accept the darkness inside of him. And maybe, if it could be shared, the burden of carrying it would not be quite so bad.

THE NEXT DAY, early in the morning, Ovi returned to the abandoned hallway. He quickly slid into the room, looking for his friend in the shadows of the room. He found her silhouetted by the glowing computer screen. Ovi walked closer, hoping to make enough noise so as not to startle Binita where she sat.

Binita greeted him. *You're back.*

You're here, he responded.

Her smile was bright again. *Thank you for coming back.*

Thank you for inviting me. Any more strange noises?

Binita shook her head. *None so far. Here's hoping it holds. But, in the meantime, let's get down to business. Look.* She pointed at the screen.

Ovi frowned as he looked closer. On the screen was a map. It was an older one detailing what looked like Northern California.

His eyes widened. *Is that what I think it is?*

Binita was practically bouncing with excitement. *Yes. The researcher we found on that paper was less than careful with their online footprint. They listed their full name and address, and it turns out that address matches another one.*

What one? Ovi's breath came quickly.

Binita grinned. *It matches an old address for an organization that filed taxes as a subsidiary of SPE.*

Walk me through it, he asked, wanting to know exactly how she worked all that out and what she wanted to do with the information. He took a seat next to her, and she filled him in. Once he was all caught up, he leaned in, examining the map on the screen again, and then he looked at Binita. *You're a genius.*

No, she blushed, looking nervously down at the keys. *I just have a lot of free time.*

Seriously, Binita. This is amazing. You are amazing. This is exactly the lead we were looking for. Kareem and the others are going to totally freak out. We can tell them, right? I guess we can tell them when we're at practice. We need to— Ovi glanced at his watch.

They were late.

He met Binita's eyes, his gaze wide. *We need to go!*

Hastily, they shut down the computer and raced into the hallway. They sprinted through the abandoned portion before slowing in the main hall. They climbed the ladder to the roof quickly and exploded onto the rooftop. Kareem, Zara, and Ashar were standing around, probably waiting for them to get started. Panting, Ovi and Binita joined them. Ovi tried to calm his heart, but between the mad dash and the excitement of the lead, his chest was pounding.

Kareem's eyes narrowed, and he folded his arms. *Where were you guys?*

Making our way here, Ovi straightened. *Why?*

Why are you late? Zara's voice was cutting, but Ovi ignored her. He glanced at Binita, wondering if now was the time to announce what she found. She took a deep breath and nodded, but she seemed hesitant. Ovi silently urged her on. He wanted her to show off because she was so smart, and he wanted the group to know it. Binita deserved this victory. If she didn't claim it for herself, then Ovi would elevate her work so that everyone would know how much she had put into finding the lead.

We found something, Binita admitted. *We think we found the location for...* She trailed off and looked nervously in Ashar's direction.

Don't worry, B, I already told him everything, Zara explained. *He's fully caught up.*

Ashar nodded with a content grin.

Oh. Okay then, Binita said, shrugging. *We think we found the location for SPE.*

Kareem's face was priceless. Shock, followed by excitement, followed by a grim determination, flashed across his features. He took one deep breath before speaking. *That's amazing, you two. How'd you do it?*

Ovi gestured to his teammate. *Binita found it.* She blushed, but he was glad that credit was going where it was due. *She found some old maps and was able to triangulate them using the address from the researcher. It's the best lead we could possibly ask for.*

Kareem frowned. *How do you know it's right?*

Shrugging, Ovi turned to his friend. *We don't, but it's all we have right now, and it's better than nothing. Which is where we were prior to this,* he added with a dry smile.

The warehouse hasn't appeared in tax records for years, Binita explained. *Which makes me think it might be abandoned. I don't know that they're hiding the missing Anunnaki there, but there must be something there that'll give us a clue at least. If it's abandoned, it's probably not that dangerous either. We can use the location to dig into some of the historical context that SPE might have. Maybe they left some records there, or maybe they left something behind that we can use.*

Kareem nodded, mulling it over. Ovi watched his friend and roommate. Kareem was a good leader despite his issues with Ashar and his extremely suppressed crush on Zara. Ovi had no doubt that Kareem would make a decision that honored not only Binita's work but the team's dedication to finding the missing Anunnaki. Ovi chose not to think about what that would mean for him and what he would need to do to support Kareem and the team on their mission.

After what felt like an eternity, Kareem spoke to the team. *Agreed. Okay. At the very least, we should prepare for recon, but if there's any hint of... something else... we need to be able to exit at a moment's notice. We're not going to try and find anyone. Not this time,* he said with a meaningful glance around the group. *The goal is for us to figure out more about why they're taking Anunnaki and whether or not they have Neelan or any of the others. Now that we know the location, we can go ahead and make a plan to enter and exit swiftly. I'm thinking that transportation will be our biggest issue, especially because we aren't supposed to leave the city. Savar and the guards will be on the lookout for us, but since we've spent so much time avoiding their radar, I imagine it will be a little easier to sneak out than it has been previously. I'll go ahead and put together an excuse that we can use to escape the notice of any of the perimeter guards. Maybe we can even—*

I can just go, Ashar cut in.

The group froze. Ovi knew his proposal was not going to go over well. His eyes bounced from Kareem to Ashar, and he waited for the fallout. Kareem did not look happy. His mouth was tight as he looked at Ashar, and Ovi's muscles twitched as he debated stepping in between them.

Excuse me? Kareem managed to grit out.

To California. I can just go. Teleport, Ashar said in a completely casual tone.

Ovi blinked rapidly.

What are you talking about? Zara asked. At least she, too, was just as confused as the others,

It's my gift, Ashar replied.

Ovi's mouth dropped open. Kareem's straightened into a tight line. Binita elicited a small gasp. Zara's eyebrows clashed together.

If Ashar could do that, truly, it would be amazing. It would protect the team and allow them to get information completely free of any risk to anyone else.

Ovi glanced at Binita, wondering if she was thinking the same thing he was and if she was remembering the terror of the ubir with the same weight he was.

So, that's it, then? Zara asked. *That's your ability?*

Ashar shrugged.

Why wait until now to tell us? Kareem questioned.

Because you're my team, and I can be useful to you.

Ovi turned to Ashar. *I thought teleporters could only go somewhere they've been.*

Maybe that's the way it is for other teleporters, Ashar countered. *But not me. I can go anywhere. At any time, too.*

Ovi's mind whirled. What Ashar was describing used so much

power that surely it was almost impossible for a student to do, much less someone who had only become a student weeks earlier.

His spine prickled. Had Kareem been right about Ashar? Was he to be trusted?

There's no way you can do that, Kareem snapped. *Stop lying to us.*

I'm not lying, Ashar replied coolly. He examined his nails as though the entire conversation was an inconvenience rather than critical to not only their survival as a team but also to accomplishing their goal of finding out more about SPE. *I can go any place. I just have to concentrate hard enough.*

There's no way that's true! Kareem practically screeched. *There are Venari who are ten times as experienced as you who can't teleport that far, not to mention to somewhere they've never been before.*

Just because your ability is pathetic doesn't mean all of ours are. Ashar smirked.

Kareem's muscles tensed, and Ovi prepared himself to jump in. He wasn't as tall as Ashar or as strong as Kareem, but he could put up a fight if he needed to. And, he hoped that if he wasn't truly threatened, he wouldn't manifest any of the darkness that he was so afraid of.

However, before Ovi needed to do anything, Zara rose.

Stop it! she shrieked. She stepped in between Kareem and Ashar, palms open to each one in a gesture meant to stop both of them. For the most part, it worked. Both Ashar and Kareem froze. Ashar's chest pressed against Zara's hand, but he took no further motions forward, and Kareem frowned at Zara's open palm. She shot scathing glares at both of them, then settled her heated stare on Kareem. *Kareem, why can't you just believe Ashar for once?*

Why would I, when what he's saying is factually inaccurate? Kareem retorted.

You don't know that! Zara's mental voice was squeaky with frustration. *And you constantly jumping down his throat isn't helping either! He's only trying to help! Maybe he has something that's different about him, and you're not willing to look past the surface because you're jealous. Grow up, Kareem. Not everyone is out to get you, and being controlling isn't going to help rescue the captured Anunnaki anytime soon!*

Ovi knew Zara and Ashar had formed a bond, but he didn't realize how strong that bond had become in such a short time. He assumed Zara, like most of the female population at the House, had been lured to Ashar by his general aura of mystery. Not only was the otherwise unflappable Zara impressed by Ashar's gift and whatever else he had shared with her over the course of their friendship, but she was also willing to step between him and Kareem in order to defend him.

Zara, who would rather not stick out her neck for anyone, was doing so for Ashar.

Kareem, Ovi nudged gently. *We're wasting time arguing about it.*

Zara's right, Binita added, *he only wants to help.*

Kareem's hands clenched and unclenched. *Let's just train. But I haven't agreed to anything. Nobody makes a move until we have more time to discuss this more.*

When? Ovi asked the question before Ashar could.

Tonight. Here. We meet back here, and we finalize the plan, Kareem spat. He didn't wait for confirmation but turned on his heel and walked off. Binita followed after him so the two of them could work on his mental conditioning.

Zara, murmuring something to Ashar, began stretching.

As Binita sat down in the corner with a still angry-looking Kareem, she looked up at Ovi. He shrugged at her before cracking his knuckles and neck to loosen his joints up. *Another thrilling adventure, I guess,* he said to himself. Binita looked as though she was thinking the same thing. It made Ovi smile a little. At least now they had somewhere they could escape to together.

CHAPTER 6

A CHANCE TO PROVE

Binita and Ovi had disappeared during their midday break, and after classes were done for the day, Kareem found out why.

When the two joined the others, they were practically overflowing with excitement. Apparently, Kareem gathered from their fervent whispers that they had spent their break tracing out different routes to the old SPE warehouse in case they were going to stick with their plan to all travel there together.

Kareem couldn't fault them for their excitement. It was the break they'd all been looking for, and while he was glad Ovi and Binita had found a lead and even happier that Binita was okay and not sneaking off to do something dangerous, he still felt isolated. Ovi and Binita had clearly bonded over their shared interest in research. Kareem watched his roommate light up as he chatted with Binita in a way he hadn't since before they all went to Canada together.

Kareem knew he should be happy. They were one step closer to finding out more about SPE and what they wanted with the Anunnaki. They were one step closer to hopefully finding Neelan. But the others had paired off, it seemed. Ovi had Binita, and Zara had Ashar. Who did he have but himself? What had he done to make it that way?

He thought about their training session on the roof earlier. Ashar had offered to use his supposed gift to teleport to SPE for them, but there was no way Kareem could trust him to, even if Ashar really had the ability to. What if it was all a lie? What if Ashar only pretended to teleport to the location and came back with false intel? He didn't know why Ashar would do it, but he couldn't be too careful. They were all going to California. Together.

The question was... how? He knew they were under more intense scrutiny than they had been prior to their Canada trip a few months ago. Even though they had spent months being model Venari students and had done every task Savar had thrown their way, it didn't mean they had free reins by any means. They couldn't leave the city boundaries, and their pictures had been sent to the guards with warning signs. If they so much as stepped outside of the boundary, they would be hauled back in front of Savar faster than Kareem could open his mouth to explain why they'd done it in the first place.

No. They needed another plan.

Kareem turned over the options in his mind. He watched as Zara rolled her eyes at Ashar, who was flirting mercilessly with an older Venari student. Binita and Ovi, heads bent over a book, whispered in hushed telepathic voices against the now normal clatter of the dining hall.

They were choosing each other. Fracturing into smaller groups. And Kareem was being left behind. He wanted to blame Ashar for the change in his team. But he knew he couldn't do that. He had been as much a factor in his isolation as Ashar had.

Kareem was the team leader. It was his job to set the pace and set the tone of how the team should operate. Instead of doing that, he had been focused on trying to out-compete Ashar.

He had been a terrible model of a leader and an even worse model of a friend.

The knowledge sat in Kareem's mind for the rest of the day. He weighed it, mulling it over until he felt sick with the heaviness of his realization.

He hadn't been modeling the team he wanted.

He hadn't even been modeling the person he wanted to be.

Kareem was still mulling this over when, without warning, while Kareem was strolling down a hallway, a Venari tapped him on the shoulder and told him Savar wanted to see him in his office.

Nervous, Kareem followed the Venari there, where he was led inside. Savar sat at his desk, working on paperwork, not even acknowledging Kareem's arrival.

Once the Venari left the office and closed the door behind him, Kareem cleared his throat to announce his presence. *Uh, Savar,* he began cautiously. *How are you?*

I was just going to ask you the same thing, Savar said with a stern glance, finally looking up at him and setting his shiny gold pen down. He gestured with a wave of his arm toward a chair on the other side of his desk. *Sit?*

It was a request, but he wasn't foolish enough to believe that it was a question.

Okay, he managed to get out. His heart galloped in his chest as he slowly sat on the edge of the hard seat.

Had Savar found out about their plan? Was the whole mission about to come crumbling down around their ears?

Waiting, Kareem gulped, his mouth suddenly dry.

So. Savar leaned forward, folding his hands on his desk. *How have you been, Kareem?*

Since the last time we talked? Fine, Kareem said as smoothly as possible under the circumstances. He hoped, anyway, that his answers seemed normal.

His nerves told another tale entirely.

Savar nodded and leaned back. *Good. That's good. I've been thinking of your team these past few days since Auraday.*

Kareem did his best not to gulp. *Oh?*

Indeed. The Auraday celebrations were quite... spirited this year, and while I enjoyed them as much as the next person, I know you all may have been experiencing somewhat of a gloom on an otherwise shining day.

Kareem breathed out. *Why's that?*

Oh, just everything, Savar waved a noncommittal hand. *I will admit you all have been surprisingly easy after the events of a few months ago.*

We told you everything we learned. You know what to do with the information better than we do. And... I risked my team, Kareem said. The last part was sincere. He remembered with crystal clarity the fear and danger they had all experienced that day. *I'd be a terrible team leader if I didn't recognize that.*

Savar steepled his fingers and stared hard at Kareem for a while before speaking. *Well. Having such insight is an excellent start to a leadership journey. Speaking of. How are you and Ashar getting on?*

If Kareem could have, he would have turned to ice. *Ashar?*

Our new student. He's on your team, correct?

Yes, he is, Kareem said slowly. *He was placed there. Without asking me first,* he added.

I needed to place Ashar in a very... well, a very particular group. I believe that of all of the teams, yours was the best fit for him.

Kareem tried to breathe around the thundering in his chest. He knew Savar had something to do with Ashar getting placed with them. Clearly, his suspicions had been accurate. Ashar was just a plant. He was someone who was reporting every little move back to Savar. He....

Savar was still talking, and Kareem frowned. *What?*

Savar tilted his head. *Were you listening?*

Um... I'm sorry I... I was distracted.

Savar huffed in irritation and leaned back. *As I was saying—Ashar's situation is such that I couldn't place him with just any of the teams. His needs are very particular, especially socially, and I evaluated all of the teams for goodness of fit. Yours was the only one that even came close, and it was a stretch. However, given the situation with your team, I thought it might work out in the end. Tell me more about how Ashar is doing so that I can evaluate the strength of my decision.*

Forgive me, Savar, Kareem said hesitantly. *What needs?*

Savar studied Kareem for a moment. *Your team,* he began slowly, almost like he didn't want to be saying it, *is strong.*

Thank you, Kareem responded automatically.

Savar nodded, then continued. *So strong, that I suppose it has made you all bored—a mistake on my part. Out of your boredom came your arrogance. Of course you went looking for trouble. You must not have enough to occupy your time with our regular coursework.*

Kareem blinked again. *I don't think I understand.*

Savar practically sneered at him. *I wanted Ashar to be with you in order to give you both something you need. Your team, a challenge, and him, a potential social group that would be a good fit. So,* he settled back in his chair again. *How did I do?*

Kareem looked at Savar, still in disbelief. Clearly, there was more to Ashar's story, as he had long suspected. What he hadn't suspected was that Savar was manipulating Ashar as much as he was trying to manipulate Kareem and his team. It appeared that, blessedly, Savar didn't know of their recent discoveries. And Ashar had been loyal, after all.

He's doing well enough, Kareem said. *Seems to have problems with authority.*

Savar nodded. *So you have that in common, then.*

Kareem wanted to grin but thought better of it. *I suppose we do.*

Well, Savar rose and gestured to the door. *Glad to see it seems to be working out so far. Ashar... he is a special case. You all are a great... fit... for each other.*

Kareem nodded, practically running out of the door. *I'll let you know if that changes,* he said to Savar.

Indeed, Savar replied. Kareem walked away, relieved he wasn't in trouble. His heart was a little lighter than it had been earlier but still laden with the new information he had just received.

It seemed that the mystery of Ashar continued. And Kareem had a decision to make.

FINALLY, at the end of the day, Kareem climbed the ladder to the rooftop with heavy feet. He was the first to arrive, a situation he had hoped for by being early. He sat on one of the large stones that made up the low wall around the perimeter of the roof, gazing out at the sun as it dipped below the horizon. When the last golden rays leached from the sky, he heard footsteps.

I thought I might find you here, Ovi's voice resonated in Kareem's mind. Kareem turned to find Ovi already seating himself on the wall next to him; Kareem hadn't even heard him come through the latched door. He'd been too lost in thought.

Oh, hey, Ovi, Kareem said with a bit of a start.

Are you okay? Ovi asked, his eyebrows scrunching together.

Sighing, Kareem picked up a crumbled-off piece of the stone and tossed it across the roof. It skittered, clacking noisily before finally resting against the side of the opposite wall. *I've been a mpumbavu.*

This, for some reason, made Ovi laugh. *You said it.*

Kareem shot him a look.

Ovi straightened up and cleared his throat. *I mean, erm, you're talking about Ashar, right?*

Yeah.

Right. So then, what are you going to do about it?

Kareem struggled to say the words despite knowing full well it was what he needed to do. *I think… I'm going to trust Ashar.*

Big move, that, Ovi's voice tone was surprised. *Are you ready for that?*

Kareem gritted his teeth. *I hope so.*

Good. Because here he comes.

One by one, the rest of the team climbed up to the roof. Zara, then Binita, then finally Ashar.

Kareem stood and faced his team. *Ashar,* he directed. *If you can do what you say, prove it.*

Ashar's eyes widened ever so slightly. *Pardon?*

Prove it.

Kareem unfolded the picture he had in his pocket, which he had ripped out of a library book for just this purpose. He opened it, showing it to Ashar and the team.

What's this? Zara asked with apprehension.

This is a meadow near my home, Kareem explained, his gaze zeroing in on Ashar again. *In it, you'll find dozens of purple flowers. Bring me back one of the flowers, and I'll let you take the lead on getting to the SPE warehouse in California.*

The team froze. Kareem waited.

Ashar's eyes narrowed. *That's it?*

That's it.

Ashar chuckled, a cocky smile on his face. He grabbed the picture from Kareem's hand. His eyes squinted as he studied the picture. *Easy.*

He turned and started walking back toward the roof's exit.

Where are you going? Kareem called.

You might want to follow me if you want your proof, Ashar called back.

I thought you could teleport.

I can.

With an irritated huff, Kareem jogged with the others to catch up to Ashar. They took turns climbing down the ladder into a very cramped supply closet, where Ashar stood in front of the closed door and put his finger to his lips to signal for all of them to keep quiet.

Why do we have to be in here? Zara asked in a whisper.

If you're playing some kind of joke on us right now... Kareem trailed off in warning.

Instead of replying to either of them, Ashar merely rolled his eyes, turned to the door of the supply closet, and opened it. Only it wasn't the House's hallway on the other side anymore. It was a meadow. One exactly like the picture Kareem had just shown them.

Ashar swiftly stepped through the door and closed it behind him.

Kareem counted. Ten. Twenty. Thirty seconds passed.

Is he coming back? Binita squeaked.

What are we still doing in this closet? Zara hissed, shoving everyone aside to climb back up the ladder to the roof. *I can't breathe in here.*

Binita and Ovi followed her up. Kareem waited just a bit longer, his gaze glued to the door, waiting for Ashar to reappear, but eventually, he sighed and went back to the roof with the others.

The first thing he noticed when his head popped through the door in the floor was the others crowded around something, laughing and gushing. Kareem quickly realized it was Ashar. He was somehow back on the roof already, the purple flower on the ground just outside their little circle.

How did you...? Kareem started, but he fell silent when Ashar held up his forearms and hands to reveal the red splotches all over them.

Stinging nettles, Ashar said coolly. *Nice touch.*

Kareem grinned, unable to help himself. *Did I forget to mention that?*

Ashar's face twisted in a snarl. *You little...*

Kareem stepped forward and offered him a little of the salve from his pocket that soothed the sting of the plant. *How'd you get back here?*

I went through the door of someone's house—maybe it was yours—and entered back here at another door. So I just climbed up from those vines like I usually do. He nodded toward the edge of the roof.

Hm, Kareem replied. He was impressed. He didn't even try to hide it as he nodded at Ashar.

Well, Kareem? Zara asked. *Was that good enough for you?*

Kareem grinned widely and reached out a hand to shake Ashar's. *Welcome to the team.*

CHAPTER 7
FRACTURED BONDS

Zara wasn't used to going places alone. Walking from the House of the Venari to the stream as though she were a loner with no friends... It didn't sit right with her, but she supposed that was just the way things were now.

She was headed to meet her team by the stream, a spot Kareem recommended, which they had been to before, to train together and plan more. Zara probably would have walked with either Binita or Ashar, but back at the House of the Venari, she unexpectedly stumbled upon an uncomfortable situation. In the hallway, just outside her room, she found herself facing Inaam and Faiza, both of whom seemed to be leaving their room at the same time as her. With no one else around and nowhere to escape, Zara nervously tucked a strand of hair behind her ear and attempted to muster a smile.

Oh hey, guys, she had said. But they didn't smile back. In fact, they stood there, blocking her path, crossing their arms, and glaring at her.

Oh, so you still remember who we are? Inaam had asked.

What are you guys talking about? If anything, Zara felt it should be herself who was hurt by them. After all, *they* had become partners. They were roommates together. It was Zara who had been shoved to the side when she was paired with Binita instead. So why could they even have the audacity to act like *she* was the evil villain here?

You're too good for us now? Is that it? Faiza asked.

I never said that, Zara retorted, her tone laced with haughtiness as she crossed her arms, her anger mounting swiftly.

It took you all of five minutes to forget about us completely, Inaam said. *Just because we were separated into different teams doesn't mean we're supposed to suddenly stop speaking to each other.*

Look, I've been busy, Zara tried. *I have a lot going on with my team.*

About that— =Faiza took a step toward her. *What have you and your team been up to? I've been hearing rumors...*

It's nothing. Whatever you heard isn't true.

Then what happened? Faiza repeated.

But Zara was too angry by then, too hurt by then. She didn't owe them anything. Not if they were going to act this way. *I've got to go,* she tried, stepping forward to see if they would move out of her path. When they didn't, she rolled her eyes. *Fine. I'll go the long way.* She turned on her heel and stalked off.

Some friend you are! Inaam called after her. Tears pricked Zara's eyes, but she forced them to stay away. She would not cry over them. Besides, she didn't need them anyway. She had Binita. And the others on her team.

Have fun with your pathetic partner. You two belong together! Faiza called. Zara balled her fist and started down a different staircase, soon no longer able to hear their voices.

Outside, the air was cool yet humid. It had rained nearly all night, and the clouds were still heavy in the sky that morning. Zara was glad her hair was up in all its braids and off her neck in a ponytail for once; otherwise, she didn't want to think about what a mess her hair would be or how sweaty her neck would be, especially when she was going to be in the presence of Ashar.

As she walked from the House of the Venari to the spot underneath the shady tree by the stream, she weaved through the lively streets bustling with people dressed in vibrant, flowing garments. The market buzzed with activity as shoppers perused the stalls, children played games, and vendors sold their goods. Rather than shove her way down the busy streets and *then* turn to the stream, Zara made her way out of the crowd and opted to walk through the grassy plains toward the outskirts of the city instead, where there was actually breathing room, following the stream to the tree.

She spotted Kareem from afar, noting that the others weren't there yet and that she was going to be the second one to arrive. He was still too far away for her to be able to tell exactly what he was doing, but he was certainly moving around a lot.

She gnawed on the inside of her cheek, her thoughts flitting to Neelan. She hated how long everything had to take. Already, so much time had passed since he first went missing. And she heard a rumor last night—she didn't know whether or not to believe it—that another Anunnaki had gone missing. If that was true, Zara worried their time was running out. She feared to think about how many other Anunnaki might go missing before she and her team had a chance to do something about it.

Zara silently acknowledged numerous qualities in Kareem that justified his role as the leader. His penchant for meticulous planning was one of them. Yet, she couldn't shake her confusion. If Ashar possessed the ability to teleport, why weren't they taking immediate action to reach Northern California and find Neelan before time slipped away?

A cough and rustling noise caught Zara's attention, causing her to quickly turn her head. In the distance, she spotted a guard partly hidden by trees and bushes, clutching his spear and avoiding eye contact. It was clear he was probably sent there to keep an eye on them. Despite their efforts, they were still under surveillance. Zara clenched her teeth and balled her fist in frustration. *How annoying!*

As she grew closer to the shady spot underneath the large tree, she realized Kareem was working out. He was in the middle of a set of push-ups, sweat dripping from his temples. The sleeves of his training uniform were pushed up to his elbows, and the legs of his pants were pushed up to his kneecaps. His eyebrows were furrowed in concentration, and as she neared him, she noticed the way he glanced at her, finished his set, and then got to his feet.

Kareem, Zara started, putting a hand on her hip and jutting her chin out at him. *We had a hard day of training already. And we're about to meet with the group to train some* more. *Don't you ever just take a break?*

He wiped his face with a towel and tossed it onto the grass beside him. Zara's gaze flickered to his muscular forearms. Kareem was incredibly fit. Sometimes, she watched him train, curious about the abs hidden underneath that uniform of his, but then she'd feel embarrassed for even thinking about it. Thinking about it now, even, she turned her head to the side and avoided looking at him any longer.

Where is Ashar? Surprised he's not with you, Kareem said. There wasn't an edge to his tone, but the way he said it so casually only made Zara more irritated than if there had been. She was trying to be nice to him, and he didn't even care. He didn't even attempt the same courtesy. And it was always Ashar these days that he brought up with her. It was always Ashar he used as a reason to fight with her.

Okay, what is your problem? Zara asked. *What did I do to you? I—*

Zara interrupted him. *No. Kareem, you are so infuriating. You just said a few days ago that you were finally welcoming Ashar as part of the team. So stop being mean. Obviously, I'm going to be seen with him now and again because he's our* teammate.

Zara.

What? she hissed.

Could you maybe... relax?

Oh. Zara noticed it then—the extra heat she was creating around them. Kareem was already sweating enough as it was. She took a deep breath and calmed herself.

Thank you, he said, wiping more sweat from his brow.

I'm just sick of your uptight attitude all the time, she said.

He sighed. *I'm sorry. I'm stressed out. And when I'm stressed out or angry, I work out. It makes me feel better. It grounds me.*

And you're stressed about Neelan? she asked, wondering if there was something else.

He nodded. *Yeah.*

We just have to act as though we're certain he's still alive, she tried. *We have to stay motivated and not lose hope. It doesn't matter how long it takes. We're going to find him.*

Of course, Zara wasn't entirely certain, but she felt compelled to say something anyway. Yet, she couldn't help but wonder why she felt this way. Why did she feel the need to lift Kareem's spirits?

Yeah, he said, clenching his jaw and looking away for a few moments before sharply turning his head back to her and nodding. *Since we're here, I wanted to ask you about what happened at the skirmish.*

Her stomach dipped, and her face grew hot. She didn't like thinking about the skirmish. She hadn't known what she was doing; she had only wanted to stop the other teams from overwhelming hers. She had been panicked. She had felt pressure to do something to stop the others since it didn't seem like anyone else on her team had any ideas of their own. Then, the next thing she knew, everyone, even the surrounding Venari watching the match, had been brought to the ground by hot, intense pressure. And she was the one making it happen, though she had no idea how.

Zara had been scared of herself then. Sitting there with Kareem, her mind flew to what Tala had told her not long ago.

Your powers might just be bigger than anything you could've imagined.

Zara didn't want to go there. Not with Kareem. Not with Tala. Not even with herself.

What about it? she asked slowly.

You sort of made an entire arena of people fall to their feet. You basically altered the atmosphere or something. You changed gravity. All of a sudden, I felt so heavy...

It was nothing, she shot out. *It lasted like a millisecond.*

Zara...

I don't know what I'm doing, Kareem. I can't control any of it. I don't know how it happened. I don't know how to make it happen again. I don't even know if I want that to happen again. Just—don't ask me about that anymore. Got it?

Don't... ask? But your abilities... Zara, we could really use them—

Just shut up, Kareem. She crossed her arms and turned away from him. As she did, she saw the rest of their teammates all walking together to join them.

That's... weird, she found herself saying. It *was* an odd sight, watching Ashar, Binita, and Ovi walk side by side, talking like the three of them had been best friends forever.

You took the words out of my mouth, Kareem agreed.

For some reason, the reclusive and quiet Ovi's facial expressions were alive with excitement as he spoke to Ashar, who nodded, apparently listening deeply. On the other side of Ovi, Binita listened to the two of them, smiling as she watched them talk.

As they grew closer, Zara began to hear their conversation.

And it's crazy, 'cause you'd think the bright red spiky balls on the plant would be enough of a warning sign, Ovi gushed.

Ashar nodded. *Oh yeah. Way worse than the stinging nettles.*

But only if you ingest it. It's not like you wouldn't have been able to walk through a field of it to pick one of the flowers to bring back. Ovi side-eyed Kareem.

I actually know a surprising amount about the castor bean plant, Ashar told him.

Ovi's face lit up. His eyes widened in disbelief. *You do?*

Yeah. I used my abilities and popped into my friend's garden once to see if I could find anything good to eat that she'd grown. Found the beans. Nearly popped a few right into my mouth. Thankfully, she stopped me in the nick of time.

I think it would take like eight of them to kill a full-grown adult. You're practically that.

Good to know a few wouldn't have completely done me in then.

I just can't believe you actually know the plant.

Finally, the three arrived to where Kareem and Zara stood. Zara smirked at the two boys. *Are you sure you don't want to be tending to the garden at the House instead of going on dangerous rescue missions with us?*

Binita giggled and caught Zara's eye, moving away from the boys to stand next to her. Zara and Binita were always together now. It had been a rough transition, to say the least—Zara knew she couldn't afford to be seen with someone like Binita if she wanted to maintain her reputation among her new friends at the House of the Venari. Back at their previous school, Binita had been unnoticed among a larger student body. Despite now training to be a Venari, she remained invisible to Inaam and Faiza. Unfortunately, Zara cared deeply about others' perceptions of her. She strived to be viewed as a confident leader, a persona she had painstakingly cultivated. Only Kareem knew the truth about her background—her life at home. Coming from the outskirts, she and her mother struggled to make ends meet in a small house in the impoverished part of the city. Becoming a Venari was crucial for Zara to provide for her mother, who suffered from a bad leg and couldn't work. Her mother was her everything, and she was all her mother had.

Zara couldn't avoid Binita forever. She knew she had to give up her original plan to keep ignoring her because she was going to be stuck with Binita for the foreseeable future. They'd become Venari together. They'd travel the world together, catching ubir together. It would be a long life if Zara had to spend it not liking Binita. So finally, she caved, and she let Binita in—albeit only a little bit. She knew Binita would eventually learn the truth about her life and her upbringing. But for now, Zara kept it a secret as best as she could. Instead, she spent her time learning about Binita, directing all the questions back at Binita, keeping the conversation away from herself. It was so unlike Zara to do so, but it was easier to just not talk about herself than to come up with all of the lies like she had at her old school.

And yes, Binita was strange. She had weird hobbies. Said weird, random things. Her gift was odd. She could be quiet one moment and outlandish the next. She was a bit unpredictable and hard to figure out, and that was saying something, considering that Zara lived with her.

Zara felt a lump in her throat as she thought about Inaam and Faiza again. She was still deeply wounded by their conversation before she left the House. How could *they* feel left behind by *her*? Because she had led their posse? Did they think she decided Binita was cooler than them? Did they think she didn't want to be their friend anymore? It wasn't true. Ever since they got separated into groups, everyone kept to their group. They sort of had to if they were going to win the skirmishes and get through training in record time—something Zara desperately wanted to do in order to start making money.

While Ovi ignored Zara's remark, Ashar smiled at her, the grin stretching across his features in the most handsome way, and instantly, Zara was flustered.

I like when you wear your hair up like that, he told her. *It looks nice.*

I didn't do it for you, she quipped with a playful sneer, although inside, she was brimming with delight. She couldn't help herself. Ashar just *oozed* coolness. And he was *so* handsome. And older, therefore smarter and more experienced. More mature. She hated that she was like all the other girls at the House who fawned over him, but she'd at least try to pretend like she wasn't. Wasn't that the best way to get a boy's attention anyway?

Oh please, she heard Kareem mutter. Then he cleared his throat. *How have the stinging nettle injuries healed?* he asked Ashar.

Ashar held up his hands. There were no traces of marks anywhere on his smooth skin. *Healed pretty much the second it happened.*

Good.

Kareem, Ovi said. *Ashar knows what a castor bean plant is.*

And?

Clearly, Ovi was still struck by awe. Zara bet Kareem hated that—Ashar had a new fan.

Next to Ovi, Ashar shrugged. *I have a friend whose ability is to grow plants. I should introduce you to her sometime, Ovi. I think the two of you would get along well.*

At this, Zara darted her eyes to Binita, wanting to see her reaction. Ashar, introducing Ovi to another girl? One who grows plants—Ovi's favorite things in the world?

Just as Zara expected, Binita cast her gaze down to her feet and was chewing on her bottom lip. It was so clear to Zara that Binita was stung thinking about Ovi and this random plant-girl. So obvious that it was annoying. Zara had only been trying to push Binita to admit to her that she had a crush on Ovi for the past two months. And still, Binita refused to tell her the truth.

All right, Kareem interjected, putting his hands on his hips and puffing his chest out authoritatively. *Now that we're all here, Ashar, why don't you go ahead and lead this thing? Tell them your ideas about California and finding the SPE headquarters.*

Ashar looked around at the others. Then he smirked at Kareem. *We know that's not what you* really *want,* he said.

What are you talking about? I said if you brought the flower back and showed us your teleportation skills, you could take the lead.

You were made the team leader for a reason, weren't you? Ashar asked. Kareem shrugged. He continued. *I'm sure you have a million ideas that you've been bursting to share with us. So why don't you just do that? I'm perfectly capable of being second-in-command. Your right-hand guy. Whatever you want. But why don't I just let you do your "leader" thing? Hey, it's just a miracle you're actually including me in something for once.*

Kareem gazed at Ashar for what felt like an eternity, seemingly unsure if Ashar's words were sincere or just playful sarcasm. It seemed as if Kareem was holding his breath, but after a while, he let it out and loosened the tension in his hands, letting them drop to his sides. *Why don't you tell us more about your abilities? I think it could be really useful.*

What else is there to say about it? I find a door. Go through said door. I'm in another place.

It's that simple? Kareem challenged.

Yeah. We can literally just pop on over to Northern California. Show me where to go, and I can get you there. We could be back within an hour if we moved fast enough.

And you can bring other people with you through the door? Binita asked.

Shouldn't be a problem.

Shouldn't? Zara repeated.

All right then, Kareem clapped his hands together. *That's what we'll do then. When the time comes. We'll teleport.*

And when is that? Ovi asked.

I don't know, Kareem muttered, shooting a glare at Ovi. Zara swiftly realized the glare wasn't directed at him. *There are still those idiots behind us, watching us,* he continued, referring to the guards. However, he refrained from gesturing toward them, fearing it might draw unwanted attention and alert the guards to their suspicious activities. *But we'll figure it out. For now, I say we get on with our training. Binita, let's run through some of those stupid—I mean helpful—mindfulness exercises together. Ashar, work with Ovi on combat. Zara, I know you can't stand taking any of my suggestions, but maybe you should work on your ability? Get angry again like you got angry at me a couple of minutes ago. Use that, see the effect you create, and see where you can take it. See how much your emotions affect your ability. Maybe that could be something Binita can help with as you progress more, too. She's great with this mindfulness stuff.*

The team broke off after Zara shot him a glare, and their training began. Zara stood by herself, pretending like she was practicing with her gift but not attempting anything to do with it whatsoever. She didn't want another scene like the one at the skirmish. She didn't want to change the atmosphere around them. She didn't want to put anyone in danger, including herself. She had her mom to think about.

Instead, she pretended like she was stewing angrily over Kareem as she watched and eavesdropped on the others. Off to the side nearest to her, Ashar and Ovi were working together, Ashar talking to him and getting to know him a bit more.

You'd get a better grip on people if you didn't have those gloves on all the time, he told him as they trained in combat while Binita and Kareem sat under the tree a little way away from them. *What's your reason for those anyway?*

Internally, a sort of alarm went off inside Zara's mind. A protectiveness came over her that surprised her a little. She watched Ovi's face, the way he decolorized and began stuttering, trying to come up with an excuse. It was clear he didn't want to tell Ashar about what he could do. He didn't want anyone to know.

Zara, Binita, and Kareem were the only ones who had seen it in action back at the warehouse in Canada when Ovi stopped the ubir from killing Binita. And ever since he did it, he'd been beating himself up about it. He hated his gift. Zara could almost relate to him about it. While she didn't think her ability could directly kill someone or hurt them in the way that Ovi was able to hurt that ubir, the power was still scary.

Ashar continued to try and get Ovi to admit to what his gift was. *Come on, just tell me. I've asked around, but it seems like everyone just makes up a different ability.*

Ashar, Zara said, stepping forward, smiling flirtatiously at him, putting on a big show of it. *That move you just showed Ovi a second ago, with the arm grab twist thing, can you show that to me? That was wicked cool.*

Ovi quickly scuttled away toward Binita, and as Ashar approached her with a friendly smile, willing and wanting to help her, Zara followed Ovi with her peripherals, watching the way he approached Binita next to Kareem, who was now giving her a death glare.

You are already pretty good with combat as it is, Ashar told her with a smile. *Are you sure you need my help?*

Definitely, Zara said, flicking her ponytail back over her shoulder. But inside, her stomach knotted. She hated the way Kareem was looking at her. Didn't he see that she was just trying to provide a distraction so that Ovi didn't have to be confronted by Ashar about his ability? She was trying to help! She wasn't being serious about the flirtation!

She wondered why she even upset Kareem in the first place. Kareem seemed to not be able to stand her most of the time. She should be able to flirt with whoever she wanted to. It wasn't like Kareem was actually jealous. That kid didn't have time for romance. He was too busy planning and plotting and being on top of the school.

She looked over at Kareem and met his eye. She tried to silently explain to him that she was just helping out Ovi, but when Kareem continued to glare at her, shaking his head, she gave up and rolled her eyes.

That boy didn't have a single romantic bone in his entire body.

They all continued practicing different things for a little while, none of them making many conversations that didn't relate directly to what they were doing. Not until eventually, when Ashar stuck his feet in the stream to cool off and turned around to the others.

The training is great and all, but is all of this really necessary? Why don't we just go into the busiest part of the city, blend into a crowd, and I'll find a door that we can all slip inside, and the guards won't even see. They'll just think we're among everyone, gallivanting around the town.

They know what your gift is, Kareem replied.

How do you know that?

If you think they don't, you're wrong. They know everything. Doesn't matter how they find out. They know. The queen probably gets told things by her advisers. And then, she has meetings with the guards and informs them of those things. That's my guess.

Ashar stroked his chin in thought for a while.

Besides, Kareem continued. *You don't understand the trouble we were in before you got here. We have to get to a point where we're no longer suspicious to them. Where Savar no longer sees us as a threat.*

Great, we're never going to rescue Neelan, Ovi said glumly.

Actually, I had a little meeting with Savar the other day, Kareem said.

At this, everyone turned to him with shocked expressions.

Zara instantly had a million questions. *Why? What about? Why didn't you tell us sooner?* It seemed like a pretty big thing to just casually tell them about now.

It was a two-minute-long conversation, Kareem explained. *He was just checking in on our team.*

Zara noticed the way his eyes flitted to Ashar for a moment before turning back to Zara. What did that mean? Did they talk about Ashar? Did Kareem learn something about him that the others didn't know?

And what did you say? Binita asked.

That everything's going well. That we wouldn't dare attempt anything so stupid again. That we gave them everything we know about SPE and are leaving it in their hands because we wouldn't jeopardize or compromise our positions here, which we are very grateful to have. He smirked. But Zara felt uneasy about it. Everything he just said was true, after all. They *did* tell Savar everything they knew. And they *did* value getting to train to be Venari. Zara didn't want to compromise her position there. But yet, she also didn't want more Anunnaki to go missing and for Savar, the queen, or whoever else to keep doing nothing about it.

He didn't say it directly, Kareem said, *but I think he's finally getting over what we did. I think he might actually believe we're not going to try anything again. But still, it's better to wait. Just in case.*

Ovi flopped down into the grass on his back, looking up at the clouded sky. Light drops of rain sprinkled their skin, but it wasn't coming down nearly as hard as it had last night. *I'm exhausted,* he said.

All right, I think we can call it a day, Kareem agreed, sitting in the grass beside him. Binita joined in, and Zara and Ashar did as well, with the five of them forming a circle in the grass. Zara picked it absentmindedly as Kareem said they should regroup before heading back to the House.

Kareem, she decided to say, *about going to California. Do you think we should wait until the next skirmish?*

To her disappointment, he nodded. *That'll be our best bet.*

But that's over a month away!

But the prize again is two days off. When else are we going to get that? We need that kind of cover.

They aren't going to fall for that twice, Binita interjected. *And that's assuming we even win again. That was hard work, the last one!*

Sure it was, Kareem said, *but was it as hard as fighting off that ubir in Canada?*

That's different, Binita said.

How?

Last time we had—

Binita stopped speaking promptly, and instantly, Zara knew exactly what she had been about to say. *We had... Ovi's gift.* Binita couldn't say that out loud without revealing a little bit more about Ovi's ability to Ashar, whom Ovi seemed not to want to tell just yet.

Anyway, Zara said loudly. *Binita is still right. If we win, they're probably going to give us a different prize. Or they're going to give us each personal escorts to follow us around our whole two days off. Make sure we don't leave.*

I know, I know. Kareem massaged his temples. Then he turned to Ashar. *You got any ideas?*

Ashar's eyes widened slightly, as if he had maybe just begun to tune into the conversation. *I got nothing,* he admitted. *I don't know enough about what happened the first time to effectively be able to plan out how to go about this second adventure with you. I'm just the newbie over here.*

Seems about right, Kareem said, looking a bit smug. *How about this: we plan to lose.*

Excuse me? Zara asked, squinting at him.

Hear me out. We lose, and one of us gets seriously hurt.

This is sounding better and better, Ovi joked with mild sarcasm.

I—Ovi, come on.

Sorry, Ovi said.

Kareem took a deep breath. *One of us gets seriously hurt, and the adults are going to think we're all sulking for a few days and tending to the person who is recovering. We're taking some personal time out of the limelight to avoid getting a bunch of hate from everyone who expected us to do so well.*

And while we're sulking, we sneak away? Ashar asked.

Yeah, Kareem replied. *One of us can stay back and keep watch. We can take turns if we have to go back multiple times. But hopefully, we don't need to. One of us stays behind, and the rest of us go. You can get us there, right Ashar?*

Uh... yeah. I can.

Why do I sense hesitation?

Have you ever *brought people with you when you teleported?* Zara asked.

I have, Ashar said quickly. *Loads of times.*

Then what is it? Binita asked.

Nothing. I mean... It's just... Not a lot of people know about my ability. And there's a reason for that. And because of this, I haven't had too many other people with me when I travel. But like I said, I'm sure it will be fine. It worked fine with two. It works great with one. I can get us to California. I can get us to that SPE address. It won't be a problem.

CHAPTER 8
IN THE QUIET SPACES

As usual, Hessa Darvish's combat training a few days later started off with brutal exercises like wall climbing, rock lifting, and jumping through controlled walls of fire, and Binita was exhausted. On top of the training she already did with her team outside of combat, along with her other classes, and helping Kareem and Zara with their mental tribulations, she was beginning to feel a bit burned out. She still longed to be a Venari, however, so she wouldn't let the burnout stop her. It was a minor setback, that was all.

After their agonizing exercises, all of the students stood around panting, holding their side-cramps, and sweating profusely. Hessa approached the front of the class and tucked her hands behind her back, her head held high.

Listen up, recruits! she shouted to everyone, drawing their attention in a single instant. *Today, we have a training exercise. And it is by no means an easy one. You and your team will practice going against another team in a combat scenario. There are three different miniature battlegrounds, one in each ring behind you. I will assign you to your areas.*

The students started looking around at each other excitedly, muttering about which team they prepared to go up against. Most of them wanted to go up against Kareem's team, of course. Everyone wanted a chance to defeat the winners of the last skirmish.

Pay attention! Hessa called. *Today's training isn't child's play. You're going to be utilizing your individual powers and combat weapons alike. There will be injury. You will cause the other team harm. But let me make this crystal clear: I won't tolerate any reckless behavior or* unnecessary *harm. We're here to learn, not to wreak havoc on each other. No injuries may be life-threatening. And only harm if absolutely necessary. The objective? Simple. Within the allotted time, the opposing teams are to go at it until the end. I will be the ultimate decider of which team of each group are the victors. This is not just about brute force, children. You need to strategize, communicate, and work together. Expect the unexpected. I might throw in some curveballs every now and again. Adaptability is key. Remember, this isn't about showing off. It's about honing your skills, pushing your limits, and becoming the best you can be.* She clapped her hands together once, the sound loud enough to reverberate through the open rings.

Great, so they were basically doing *more* skirmishes, just miniature versions. Binita internally groaned. She was not looking forward to this. She didn't feel confident her ability was anything good enough to be used in combat. Being able to change her head into other people's, along with her voice to match theirs, was something more fit for subtle, sneaky attacks against opposing offenders, not during a fight.

Now, Hessa continued. *I have to break you up a little to try and make the teams more even. But out there in the field, you might come across some instances where you have to work with other Venari and not just your partner or team. So, it's always good to adapt and mend your ability to work with others. With that being said, the first ring will have*

Aisha Ngozi, Malaika Toure, and Dakarai Abebe going up against Binita Chudasama, Zara al-Hazmi, and Ovi Fadel.

Binita quickly met Kareem's gaze, surprised. Suddenly, they were without a team leader. Were Kareem and Ashar still going to be prepared to work together against another group?

Idris Lajami, Kareem Maamaoum, and Ashar Kouri will go up against Mira Moyo, Caden El Tain, Inaam Kirdar, and Faiza Shahd.

But that's three against four! Kareem complained.

Hessa merely nodded. *Glad to see you know how to count, Kareem.* She smirked at him and then looked at everyone else as she announced that the last ring would contain Tarun Munir, Temi Bello, and Ekon Eze against Veer Lapido, Aryan Nenge, Samira Okoye, and Jalla Zivai—apparently, that was the only group that would get to stay together. Binita wondered why that was. Were the groups chosen at random, or did Hessa have a specific reasoning for wanting to pair the groups the way she did?

Now go! Hessa shouted, and everyone broke up into their teams and settled into the three rings in the order of how she read the teams out.

How are the three of us supposed to take on them? Zara hissed in Binita's ear, clearly frustrated.

Biting her bottom lip, Binita shook her head. *I have no idea.*

Binita looked down at her opponents on the other side of their ring. Aisha, the first girl with a heavier build and an innocent, childlike expression on her face, nodded repeatedly, as if one of her teammates was telling her about their plan of attack. Next to her, Malaika Toure pounded her fist into her hand, smiling at Binita and her team. Binita didn't know what Aisha's power was, but she did know Malaika's—she had the ability to cause nonliving objects to spontaneously burst into flames upon touching them.

Last, there was Dakarai Bebe, who was made fun of often because his ability was to make his hair rapidly grow, and he had yet to find much use for it.

On the other side of the battlefield, each team had its own chest full of weapons to choose from. Zara pulled out a sword. Binita went for a stave like the one she used in the last skirmish. Ovi picked up not only a sword but also a wooden shield. Binita wondered if she should've grabbed one of those as well. What if Aisha, the one whose powers were unknown, could do something super dangerous? Maybe Ovi already knew what her power was, and that's why he was preparing himself.

Before Binita could go back to the chest to grab a shield, Hessa blew into some wooden whistling device that sounded loudly across all three rings, and then she shouted, *Begin!*

In a panic, Binita's eyes darted back and forth between Zara and Ovi. What was their plan of attack? What were they going to do? Just run at the other team with no organization? She wished dearly she had Kareem there to coach them along. She hadn't realized how valuable he was as a team leader until that moment.

Ovi shrugged at her with wide eyes and raised his shield to cover as much of himself as he could while the other team charged at them.

Someone in the ring next to them laughed, and Binita turned her head to find Idris eyeing down Ovi with a sinister smile on his face. *Glad I'm not on* your *team,* he said. *Towering behind a shield like a baby. Why don't you just take your gloves off, Ovi? Show us your powers.* He was completely unfazed by his opposing team attacking. People tended to stay away from Idris because they feared being controlled by him. Not to mention, he was a bully.

Binita quickly dodged someone's throw of a spear and rolled in the dirt before jumping back up to her feet. She wasn't interested in fighting back against the other team. She was interested in protecting Ovi.

Why don't you go help your teammates? Ovi called to Idris, but his voice was soft. It lacked confidence or threat.

Binita noticed Zara fighting against Aisha with her sword,

easily able to do so while also watching the interaction between Idris and Ovi. Then suddenly, her sword slipped out of her hands and turned into a gooey, almost jelly-like substance on the ground.

So that was Aisha's power? Turning things into jelly-like substances?

Zara growled in irritation and dodged the swing of Aisha's sword. It seemed to Binita like it was more of an inconvenience to Zara than it was actually scary that Aisha was coming at her with it. She admired Zara's bravery.

Why don't you tell us what your power is, Ovi? Idris continued, manipulating someone from the opposite team right as they lunged at Idris, causing them to halt with their sword raised in the air.

Shut up, Ovi said, defending himself against Malaika's advances. She was trying to touch Ovi's shield to make it burst into flames.

I bet it's something stupid, Idris continued. Why wouldn't he focus on his own battle? Why did he find right now a good time to tease Ovi?

Something soft snaked around Binita's ankle, and she looked in time to see a mane of hair tied into a knot around it. She didn't have time to react before she was pulled to the ground. She hadn't realized Dakarai had learned to control the *way* his hair grew, to manipulate it into moving in certain ways. She should've paid better attention in class. She always paid attention to everything. Better than everyone else did.

Binita fought the hair off while Idris kept at it. *Let me guess... butterfingers? You keep the gloves on because otherwise, everything you touch slips right from your grasp?* He cracked up at his own joke, ducking from somebody's swing and cackling.

That's it!

The next thing Binita knew, Zara was knocking her opponent to the ground with a swift maneuver, stealing her sword from her, and running out of her ring and into the next one. She was headed right at Idris.

Caught off guard, unable to see her coming in time enough to stop her with his manipulation, Zara swung at him with the sword, and he barely had time to duck.

I bet you only think Ovi's ability is something stupid because, in reality, you know it's probably something better than any of our gifts combined! she shouted at him as Hessa blew into her wooden whistle again. Everyone stopped fighting at once, and Binita looked over at an angry-looking Hessa as she marched toward the scene.

Binita jogged toward Zara. *Stop!* she called to her. *Zara, don't say anything else!* She reached Zara and pulled her away from Idris, who continued smiling like this whole thing was amusing to him. His equally awful best buddy, Caden, joined his side with a matched facial expression, wanting in on the fun, apparently.

Better than any of our gifts? he asked, raising an eyebrow. *What is it then? Midas touch?*

Behind them, Ovi sunk back, glaring.

That's enough, Hessa said, reaching the center of all of the students, standing closest to Idris and Zara.

Can you read people's thoughts by touching them?! a girl's voice called from somewhere. Binita couldn't tell who asked it.

Does he kill people by touching them or something?! a male voice called from even further away, likely at the other end of the third ring.

Binita slapped a hand to her forehead. This was not good.

She turned around to Ovi, whose expression darkened and shoulders slumped forward. Then he stormed out of the ring and into the shadows of the lower level, leaving the class entirely.

ONCE COMBAT TRAINING WAS OVER, and it was time for their midday break, Binita scanned the entire dining hall for Ovi since it was typically where all of the students gathered, despite them not needing to eat often. Ovi was nowhere in sight. However, Binita was determined to find him. She was deeply worried about him, wondering if he thought everyone must've figured out what his powers were after that last kid yelled out that thing about him killing people during training. But it wasn't like Ovi *killed* people. He could get close, sure. But nothing had been confirmed after Ovi stormed out of the ring. Ovi had to know that.

Binita was about to leave the dining hall when a hand grabbed her elbow, and she whirled around, facing a worry-eyed Zara.

Are you looking for Ovi? Zara asked, visibly chewing on the inside of her cheek.

Yeah, have you seen him?

No. He wouldn't even look at me in class. I... I was only trying to help, Binita.

Binita was the only one who had ever seen this side of Zara. In fact, Binita was pretty sure even Zara's other friends, the ones she arrived at the House of the Venari with, Inaam and Faiza, didn't get to see it. Binita saw the *real* side of Zara. The softer side. Not the facade she put on in front of everybody else.

I understand that, but it just made more of a mess of things, Binita explained to her.

Well, duh, I realize that. I was trying to do the right thing. Just like the other day with Ashar.

What about Ashar? Binita asked, tilting her head.

Zara looked around to make sure no one was overhearing them. Then she turned back to Binita. *When I pretended to flirt with him to get him to stop asking Ovi about his ability. I could tell Ovi didn't want to talk about it. So, I provided a distraction.*

Binita smiled at the nice gesture. *I was wondering why you wanted Ashar's help with your fighting skills when you're already really good at it.*

Yeah. I'm sure Kareem was wondering the same thing. He was not pleased to see it.

He's never pleased to see you conversing with Ashar.

I know. What is that? I just don't get it.

I think he's starting to come around to Ashar. A little bit more every day. Especially with them having to team up without us in combat today.

After Ovi left combat training, the battles resumed, with Zara and Binita losing pitifully against their team. But Ashar and Kareem worked incredibly well together despite having Idris on their team. They won against their opponents—naturally.

I hope, Zara said. Well, if you see Ovi, can you just apologize to him for me? But don't say, "Zara wanted me to tell you she's sorry." Say something else, like, "I'm sure Zara feels bad about what happened and didn't mean to upset you." Or, I don't know, tell him to not be such a big baby.

Do you want to come with me to look for him? Binita asked. Maybe you can tell him... that... yourself.

Zara tossed her long braids back. *No thanks. I actually haven't eaten in forever, and I think I'm going to help myself to a real meal for once.*

Binita nodded but didn't move to leave Zara, who seemed to sense there was something else Binita wanted to talk about.

What is it? Zara asked.

Have you thought about what Ovi is so afraid of? Binita blurted out.

What do you mean?

You know—why he came to hate his ability so much.

Zara shrugged. *Not really. He's just scared of it.*

But I think something had to have happened because he doesn't seem scared—he seems traumatized.

Zara simply stared at Binita with an "I don't know what to tell you" look, so Binita sighed, and they said their goodbyes.

Binita spent all of her midday break searching for Ovi with no luck. She saw him again only after classes were done for the day, and he was rushing toward the massive doors of the exit.

Not knowing whether or not Ovi would appreciate having her company, Binita decided to follow him. She was good at this kind of thing. She was small and stealthy and could easily hide. She didn't interrupt Ovi as he walked ahead of her, mostly because he was too far for her inner voice to reach him, but also because she wanted to know where he was headed before she made the decision to announce her presence or not.

As Ovi darted into the Rhapta library, Binita smiled a little. She should have figured he'd go there.

She entered the library shortly after he did, but Ovi was nowhere in sight, lost among the stacks of old books.

Stealthily, she crept along the aisles in pursuit of him, worried about his whereabouts and wondering what he was up to. Finally, as she turned a corner, she found a secluded table in the back. Quickly making herself unseen, she cautiously peered around the corner to observe his actions.

She should have known. Ovi wasn't up to anything suspicious. He was simply sitting at a table, a book about plants cracked open in front of him. His eyebrows were furrowed as he stared at the pages, and one of his feet bounced anxiously under the table. Binita smiled softly as she watched him, but her worry lingered. Was he genuinely engrossed in the words on the pages, or was his mind still entrenched in the combat scene within the rings?

It took her only a moment to decide that she didn't care if he discovered she was following him. She made her presence known and approached him swiftly. He offered a feeble smile upon noticing her, and she could tell he wasn't in the mood for company. Returning to his book, he silently indicated that she should leave him be.

But she couldn't simply walk away. She wanted to help him.

Without a word, she lightly nudged his bicep with her elbow and motioned with her head for him to accompany her. She hoped to whisk him away somewhere to lift his spirits, and she had a pretty good idea of how to do so.

He shook his head at her, appearing apologetic for refusing, and resumed his reading.

I suppose he'll need some more coercing, Binita thought to herself. Leveraging her gift, she morphed her appearance into Kareem's. With Kareem's authoritarian, try-hard voice echoing from her mind, she addressed Ovi, violating the internal speaking volume rules of the library. *Ovi. You have obligations to fulfill as part of this team. You need to join me. Now.*

Come on, "Kareem," Ovi protested playfully, though his moodiness still lingered. *You're risking us getting kicked out.*

Fine, Binita retorted in Kareem's voice before switching to Zara. Mimicking Zara's snootiness, she tapped her foot and jutted her chin out, tossing her braids over her shoulder. It was fun to play with Zara's braids. *Seriously, Ovi. You're being annoying. Just come with me. You're not too cool to be seen with me; we all know that.*

Finally, Ovi cracked a smile. Shaking his head at her, he seemed on the verge of following her, but instead, he returned to his book.

So she switched to Ashar's head. *Oh, come on, Ovi-man. You really should join me. I'm going somewhere cool. Because I'm cool. And confident. I promise you won't regret it.*

Ovi laughed, warming Binita's heart. She relished bringing a smile to his face; he always seemed so moody around others. She cherished being one of the few who could evoke such a reaction from him and being one of the few to witness it.

Going back to her true self, she asked, *So, will you come with me already?*

He sighed heavily. *I suppose.*

Excitedly, she grasped his gloved hand with both of hers, pulling him out of his chair. They practically sprinted out of the library, with him protesting the entire way.

Once they stepped back outside into the setting sun, she turned to him. The golden rays of the sun illuminated her while Ovi stood as a dark, pouty shadow.

I think you just need to be outside, she told him. *We don't even have to talk much. Sometimes, just being outdoors can be incredibly healing.*

He shrugged. *If you say so.*

She smiled at him, not caring that he didn't return it. *I'm just going to say two things about it, and then I won't talk about it anymore.*

Binita, I don't want to talk about what happened earlier, said Ovi.

Two things! Binita cried. He grimaced but waited. *Nobody figured out what your gift is. The talking about it stopped as soon as you left. Hessa forced us to resume our skirmishes, and no one said another word that wasn't directly related to the activity. So you don't have to worry about that. And also, Zara really only wanted to help you. I know she's conceited and doesn't always realize her way of helping sometimes does more harm than good. But I promise you, she feels bad, and she's going to be more careful.*

He crossed his arms and stared at her, saying nothing.

Well? she asked.

Is that it? he replied.

Yes! She grabbed his gloved hand again and pulled him along excitedly through the bustling citizens of Rhapta.

Binita, where are we going? Ovi asked, chuckling a little bit, which fueled Binita's continued excitement.

Where is your favorite place to spend your time? she called over her shoulder as they meandered through the crowds and turned down various streets and alleyways.

The library! That place that you just yanked me out of!

I figured! She finally stopped running with him as soon as they were out of the main streets, on the outskirts of the city, where it was quieter, calmer, and more scenic. *But is that it? Come on, there's got to be somewhere else you like to go. Show me.*

He seemed to think about it for a moment, grabbing the back of his neck. *I don't know, Binita...*

Come on! You're a plant lover! You can't tell me that you only like to read *about them.*

Fine. He sighed. *We're already headed in the right direction anyway.*

He stepped past her, brushing against her arm as he did so, sending goosebumps rippling down her skin, and he started leading the way. They no longer ran. This time, they casually strolled, Binita walking alongside him. The two of them were comfortably quiet until they arrived at exactly the kind of place Binita pictured Ovi to be infatuated with.

Near the barrier, secluded behind trees and bushes, was a small garden inside an iron-gated square. He opened the iron gates, and it squeaked with rust, and Binita stepped inside, a wide smile on her face.

It's not mine, Ovi explained. *I just found it one time; I'm not even sure who tends it. But yeah.* He sat down on a stone bench in the center of it all, leaving enough space beside him so that Binita could sit, too. When she did, she found herself surrounded by a wide variety of colorful flowers and plants, and she was pretty certain she had never seen anywhere so beautiful in her entire life. And to think, it was right here, inside the barrier of Rhapta.

I've done a lot of exploring, but I've never seen anything like this, she admitted to Ovi.

That one's a king protea, he said about a giant flower with spiky, pointed pink and yellow leaves and a massive white center. *Doesn't smell all that great, but it's beautiful, isn't it? They're super resilient and can withstand extreme climate changes.*

I love it, Binita said.

He pointed to a patch full of small white, purple, yellow, red, and yellow flowers all mixed together. *And those are Livingstone daisies. Also known as ice plants. See the way the sun hits it? How they look a tiny bit icy?*

Binita nodded.

It's not ice. It's actually tiny little hairs on the plants that reflect light. It makes it look like that.

I've seen those around. I've always wondered what that was.

Or there is the Impala lily. He pointed out what looked to be tree branches with red and white flowers poking out of the end of them. *They grow better in places like this, where it's more tropical. They grow great indoors, too. They make good bonsai plants. But they're also poisonous. Sometimes, they're used to poison the tips of arrows. And it makes a good fish stunning potion to make catching food easier.*

How do you have the time to learn all of this?

I had all kinds of time before I became a Venari pupil.

I'm sad that I didn't really know you before this. I think we could've been friends a long time ago.

He shrugged. *We're friends now?*

She moved just the tiniest bit closer to him. For a while, he stayed still, but then, to her disappointment, he slid the tiniest bit away from her. Binita didn't take personal offense; she knew he was just nervous about getting too close to people because of his power.

Binita opened her mouth to ask him something about it, but he quickly cleared his throat and resumed talking about the plants. *Oh, and look at this one.* He stood up and walked a few feet away, so Binita followed. *This is the bell stapelia. It's a pretty common flower outside of Rhapta, but here, it was modified. It has magical properties, but only inside Rhapta. See this giant opening?* He pointed at the massive circular hole of the bell-shaped flower. The plant grew sideways as though the bell part was lying on its side among the leaves around it. This allowed for things to be inserted into the hole.

No one knows how it works or when it started, but if you place tiny insects inside of the flower, the flower will duplicate them. But it only works with insects.

I'd like to see that!

Insects—now *that* was something that interested Binita.

Ovi snickered, as if he knew she would say something like that.

So, Binita asked, casually wandering around the rest of the garden, taking in everything else. *How long ago did you find this place?*

Well, once I was tapped, I tried to be out of the house, away from my aunt and uncle, more and more.

She turned to face him and saw the look of sadness in his eyes. *Why?* she asked, stepping toward him. But then she remembered—she was supposed to be cheering him up! This kind of conversation was not going to do the job! She could figure out the whys and hows of his life later on when he was more open to talking about it. Right now, she could tell he still wasn't interested.

I mean, never mind. She shook her head repeatedly. *It's my turn to show you some of* my *hiding spots.*

Oh yeah? He raised an eyebrow, intrigued.

Consider yourself lucky, Ovi Fadel. Because I don't show these to just anyone.

With a smile, she led the way out of the garden.

First, she led him to one of the many fountains spread around the city. This one, in particular, sat just behind their old school, on the road between that and a cluster of houses. It was a smaller one, not as often visited or used as a meeting place as other fountains around the city were. But Binita liked this one.

I don't get what makes this so secret, Ovi said when they arrived at it. He reached his hand out and let some of the water spray fall onto it. It beaded up and rolled off; his glove was water-resistant. To her amazement, he took the glove off and again stuck his hand under the water to feel the spray. She didn't want to make it a big deal by staring too long, so she looked away and explained herself. *When you sit at this exact spot, just over here—* she walked around the fountain, to the east side of it, partly obscuring her vision of Ovi behind the water spray. *And lean in, like this—* she leaned toward the fountain, her head tilted, sticking an ear out. Ovi followed her to see her more clearly, putting his glove back on. *You can hear people talking. Voices carry almost like magic. I can hear conversations people* definitely *meant to keep private.*

She motioned for him to try it, and he did so eagerly.

I hear one now! Ovi called with a grin. *That husband and wife over there are fighting about the husband's foul-smelling shoes and how he needs to do something about that before she makes him sleep outside.*

Together, they started laughing. *Finally,* Binita thought. *My plan is working. I'm cheering Ovi up!*

After they left the fountain, Binita led him to her next secret spot. She was certain she couldn't be the only one who knew about it, but she gathered only a select few did. And with her adventurous nature, she got to be one of the few.

What are we doing? Ovi asked in a whisper as they stood behind the Grand Hall. He looked uneasy, checking their surroundings as though he was worried about getting caught by someone.

There's a secret entrance into the Grand Hall back here, she whispered.

Why do you know that? he asked with an exasperated sigh.

Because, she said with a giggle, *all you have to do is wiggle between these two hedges and then move the metal grate.* She showed him by doing just that, wedging herself between two thick hedges, disappearing from sight for Ovi. *Come on!* she called out to him in her head. Soon enough, he joined her, and they were cramped together in front of a metal gate, completely hidden from the rest of the town. Together, they heaved the heavy grate to the side and found a square hole wide enough for them to crawl through one at a time.

I'll go first, Binita started.

We don't have to go in, Ovi said.

Come on.

She led the way, and although she sensed some reluctance, Ovi followed. The secret crawlspace was long and damp and cold, the stone chilling Binita as her hands and knees pressed down on it while they crawled. It would be pitch-black in there if it weren't for the bioluminescence that somehow glowed along the walls from a moss-like plant in shades similar to aurelius borealis. That was Binita's favorite part about the secret tunnel.

I've read about these! Ovi gasped. *I've never seen it in person!*

I knew you'd like it.

At the end of the tunnel, they found themselves at another grate.

This is the only tricky part. She spied around through the squares of the metal, and once she knew the coast was clear, she pushed the grate down, and it landed with a loud clang onto the stone flooring of the men's bathroom.

The two of them crawled out quickly and put the grate back just in time before a man walked in and gaped at Binita standing there.

Oops! I can't believe I walked into the wrong one! she cried loudly before running out.

Seconds later, Ovi joined her, laughing hard and clutching his side. *You're ridiculous, you know that?*

I usually don't get seen by anyone, she explained with a shrug. Normally, she'd be much more embarrassed, but with Ovi, for some reason, she wasn't. She didn't feel so self-conscious. She liked spending time with him.

Did you see that guy's face? Ovi asked.

Binita merely smiled and watched Ovi laugh, glad to see him happy. Then she said, *Okay, one more place.*

She led the way through the Grand Hall, getting stares from many people since she and Ovi were in their Venari training attire and had no business being in the Grand Hall. She waved to Hamidi, one of the event security guards, as they walked out the front and down the massive steps. On the trek to her last hiding spot, she also stopped by one of the food stalls to say "hi" to Faraji, a sweet old lady who sold everyone's favorite sweet treat, steamed lemon buns.

And then they stumbled upon Mosi, a healer who once came to her family's home to help her older sister, Kofi, with a snake bite from an African spitting adder. The snakes were indigenous to Rhapta, and their venom was the only one in existence that slowed the Rhaptans' natural healing abilities. Mosi and Binita stopped and chatted for a few minutes as Ovi waited patiently nearby.

How do you seem to know so many people? Ovi asked as they resumed walking afterward. *And why are they all so much older than you?*

Do you mean to ask me why my only friends seem to be adults?

Maybe. He smiled at her innocently.

She shrugged. *Hamidi has helped me many times in the Grand Hall, whether he wants to or not. Whether I want him to or not. And Faraji, come on—how could you not want to be friends with the woman who makes the most delicious treats in the world?*

True.

And for Mosi, they're a family friend.

I see. I didn't know you were so sociable.

It depends on who I'm around. A lot of people I just meet because I'm in the right place at the right time. People get curious about me because I am such a loner. But I'm not your average loner; I'm one of those loners who goes out and about in the world, letting everyone see what a loner she is. I think that's why adults like to talk to me. They get curious. I don't know. I guess I never really felt like I fit in with people my age.

You're more mature, Ovi agreed.

So are you.

I don't know about that.

We're both old souls, she joked. She nudged him playfully as they walked, and to her surprise, he didn't immediately flinch away from her. That had to be a good sign, right?

And last but not least, she said as they approached one of the very few remaining abandoned, crumbling homes in southern Rhapta. The building was so deteriorated that it was basically entirely outdoors, and it could be entered from three out of four sides because of what little walls remained. But the one small portion where the roof collapsed but was held up by a small half wall allowed the tiniest opening for Binita to crouch and step through. Ovi followed her, and they found themselves in what used to be the kitchen. They couldn't exactly stand, but they didn't have to crawl, either, so hunched over, Binita led the way to a row of cabinets, where she could still wedge one open with a lot of effort. And when she did, she revealed to Ovi her curio collection.

Something tells me these weren't left with the house, Ovi replied when he looked at it all.

You'd be correct, she said, admiring her collection.

What even is all of this?

My collection, she said simply.

And how did you come to have these "collectibles?" He put air quotes around the word "collectibles" as he internally said them. Binita didn't take offense. One man's trash was another man's treasure. She was well aware she liked weird things. She was also aware that he didn't actually seem to care that much about her strange hobby. He wasn't the judgmental type.

Well, this one—she picked up the vintage pocket watch—*I found one day on the outskirts. Just lying there. Waiting for me. I like to think it belonged to a legendary explorer, one who, like me, knew all of the hidden passages throughout Rhapta.*

You know all of them? Ovi asked, sounding skeptical.

Well, no, but I want to. She picked up a small bag and untied the drawstring, dumping the two dice inside of it onto the palm of her hand. They were carved out of red and purple gemstones. *These were used by the Elders way back when they used ancient divination rituals to predict the outcomes of important events.*

How did you get them? he asked. *Don't they belong on a display somewhere?*

I was in the right place at the right time, she said again. It was better than admitting she stole them.

Fine. How about the feathers? You and your feathers, he said with a headshake, smiling fondly at her.

There's nothing really special about them. I just like them. And I think all of the colors go so well together, don't you? She had her feathers arranged in a small vase inside the cabinet. She never plucked them off birds directly; she only picked up the ones they left behind.

She picked up the item next to the vase. *But this, this was my older brother's. I took it from him. He never liked it anyway. One of his old teachers gave it to him, and supposedly, it's carved with symbols of protection to ward off negative energy and bring good luck. But he claimed it did the opposite. Probably because his girlfriend broke up with him the day after he got it. But if you ask me, he was lucky that that happened. She was horrible.*

Ovi chuckled.

She showed him the other items. The wooden flute she got from Mosi, who gifted it to her and told her it was carved from the city's sacred trees and it played only haunting music. Binita didn't play it for Ovi because she didn't want to bring the mood down. She then picked up a doll with missing eyes that thoroughly creeped Ovi out, and Binita didn't disagree. It had creeped her out, too, when she found it abandoned in a hidden alleyway. It was deeply unsettling, and Binita had always wondered where it came from, why its eyes were missing.

She also had a necklace made from human teeth. It was strung together with twine, and all the teeth were various shapes and sizes, like they didn't all come from the same mouth. She traded a sketchy man at the market for it, giving him her handmade beaded necklace she made herself when she was five. She didn't know what she was supposed to do with it, but he wanted her necklace, and she was curious about the teeth, so she accepted his offer.

You don't worry that someone's gonna find all of this and take it? Ovi eventually asked.

If you came across a strange collection like this, would you want to have anything to do with it? she asked back, which made Ovi laugh.

I guess not.

Yeah, I think my collection is safe.

So, you just like to go off and explore on your own? he asked next. *You must've spent a great deal of your childhood outside to know about all these places.*

I did. I do. I... I guess I have a bit of middle-child syndrome.

What do you mean?

The second youngest of seven. I'm forgotten about all the time. Especially since I'm nothing special. I'm not super pretty. I don't have an incredible gift. I'm just... me. So I just got used to being alone. I started to prefer it that way.

Binita, you can't seriously say that, he argued instantly.

Say what?

That you're nothing special.

Why? It's the truth.

You couldn't be more wrong.

Binita's stomach fluttered. But Ovi didn't know what it was like to grow up in the house that Binita did. He wouldn't understand.

Anyway. It's awfully cramped here, don't you think? she asked, squeezing past him and leaving her curiosities behind. She heard the sounds of him closing her cabinet for her, and then he followed her out.

Binita, I was trying to tell you something.

What? she asked, her heart skipping a beat.

I... I think you're special.

You do? She peeked at him through underneath her lashes.

He cleared his throat. *Yeah.* When he broke eye contact, Binita was disappointed. *I mean, you're training to be a Venari. How many of your siblings can say that?*

True.

She tried to start walking, but he stopped her, calling out to her, momentarily grabbing her with his gloved hand before quickly pulling it away. *Why do you want to be a Venari?*

Isn't it obvious? she asked bitterly. *I want to feel important. I want to feel like I matter. Since my family never made me feel that way.*

CHAPTER 9
BETWEEN TWO WORLDS

Ashar had been hoping to catch only one or two of his group members hanging out in the dining hall during their midday break so that he'd only have to break the news to one of them, and let *that* person be the one to tell the others. Instead, he happened upon all four of his teammates sitting together at a table, looking as though they were waiting for him to join.

There he is, Binita called, the first one to notice him approaching.

Dang it, Ashar thought to himself as he straightened up and nodded at them. They weren't going to like this.

He stood in front of the table, but he didn't make any moves to sit down, even though there was a clearly vacant spot next to Zara, who looked up at him expectantly.

We're having a team meeting tonight on the roof, Zara told him, playing with her braids and giving him a friendly smile. One that she never gave Kareem. Not when Ashar was around.

Ashar's stomach dipped nervously. *Actually, I'm not gonna be able to make it to the meeting tonight.*

You're joking, right? Kareem asked loudly. Ashar met his eyes, and a piercing stare greeted him.

I wish I was, Ashar tried. *I just have something I have to do.*

What is it? Binita asked, which was surprising to Ashar. Binita didn't usually ask for details about anything. But yet, Binita somehow always seemed to know so much.

Ashar scratched the back of his head. *Uh...*

Aren't you at least going to sit down now? Zara asked. *So we can discuss things here if you won't be around later?*

No, I can't, he replied. It didn't matter how angry they got at him; this wasn't something he could change his mind about.

Whatever, Zara said, tossing her braids over her shoulder and scooting down on the bench to take up more space and make it clear there was no longer any room for Ashar.

No, not "whatever," Kareem replied. *What's the big idea?* He glared at Ashar. *You fought so hard to get acceptance into our group, and now you're pulling this?*

It's not a big deal, Kareem, Ashar protested. *It's one meeting. You guys can fill me in. There's no need to overreact.*

Instead of replying, Kareem stayed still, glowering at him. Ovi sat silently beside him, grimacing like he knew Kareem was going to flip out about Ashar the second Ashar walked away, badmouthing him to everyone. Binita merely eyed Ashar down, not looking quite angry but not looking pleased, either. If anything, she was curious. He had the feeling she wanted to follow him, so he'd have to keep an eye out for that.

At least tell us why, Kareem said.

It's a long story, Ashar replied, shoving his hands in his pockets. *It's just this once.*

He didn't want to have to explain it to him. To any of them. If he told them where he planned on being tonight, then he'd have to get into his whole life story and talk about his past with them. But

Ashar didn't really care to do that. Especially not with them; he wasn't even sure if they really liked him or not.

In reality, it was his uncle's birthday. And he couldn't miss it.

Guys, who cares? Zara asked, bugging her eyes out at everyone and talking loudly inside their heads. *We don't need him to have the meeting. Just let him go.*

I'll see you guys later, Ashar said before he turned and walked away from the group. Sure, maybe it would be easy to just explain that it was his uncle's birthday. But he didn't want them asking questions. He wasn't ready to let them into that part of his life. Ashar and his uncle moved from the outskirts of Rhapta to the formerly abandoned southern quarter. They took residence in one of the previously abandoned homes that had sat in ruin for decades. It had been built back up nicely enough, but it still wasn't anything compared to some of the exquisite homes around the city. But it sure was a heck of a lot better than the outskirts had been. Before the move, Ashar and his uncle lived in what was practically a shack. Uncle Adil, who had no ability and was a man of few words, picked up odd jobs whenever he could to support his nephew. Ashar's parents died when he was only two, passing away within weeks of each other. Ashar hardly remembered them. Just fragmented glimpses of memories. Flashes of them smiling at him behind his eyelids at the most random moments. But he loved and respected his uncle and would be forever grateful he had been so willing to take him in as just a small boy.

In more recent years, his uncle had gotten too old to work as many odd jobs as he used to, so Ashar had been doing everything he could to make life easier for the old man. If that meant sneaking around the city and sometimes stealing things—okay, *oftentimes*—then so be it. It was like his best friend Nasrin told him—becoming a Venari was a good thing for so many reasons, one of them being able to support Adil. Adil had supported Ashar for all those years of his life. Ashar hated it when Nasrin was right.

Ashar.

A figure stepped in front of Ashar, blocking the exit of the dining hall right as he was about to leave. He stepped back and smiled at Faiza, who stood before him, running a hand over her shorn hair while giving him a flirtatious smile.

Where are you off to? Do you maybe want some company?

Ashar was used to getting this kind of attention now. A lot of the girls in their Venari training class talked to Ashar that way. He was older than the majority of his Venari training group, and for some reason, that made him all the more intriguing.

Ashar was usually suave and smooth about these kinds of interactions, but Faiza had been so blunt that he was slightly caught off guard.

Oh... he trailed off. *Think,* he told himself, racking his brain for a way to let her down easily.

I just... I saw you leaving, Faiza continued, *and I was headed out too, anyway. So I figured maybe you and I could hang out.*

He watched her look to her left, and he quickly realized that Inaam was watching their every move. Ashar wondered if Inaam pushed Faiza into doing this. Or if they had some sort of bet. He wouldn't put it past them. They liked to try to talk to him any chance they had.

Unfortunately, Faiza, I am in high demand, Ashar explained with a smart smile. *I could've hung out with you, but you would've had to book time with me more in advance.* He winked at her and gave her a friendly shoulder tap. *But maybe next time. You know how much I love spending time with you.*

What was her ability again? Was she the one who weighed as much as an elephant, even though you'd never guess by looking at her? He reminded himself not to get on her bad side, or else he might get crushed by her.

Oh, okay then, Faiza replied, her face falling.

Ashar started to walk past her.

Just let—let me know when you're free again! she called to him. He didn't look back. Instead, he snickered to himself as he walked through the halls of the House. It was just too fun. He didn't mean to lead the girls on, but he thoroughly enjoyed the extra attention. *Nasrin would be choking back vomit if she witnessed that exchange between Faiza and me,* he thought to himself with another chuckle. Nasrin was his favorite person in the entire world. He missed her terribly and hated they were no longer in school together. It had been a while since he'd seen her, which wasn't good. He needed to make arrangements soon, or else he'd never hear the end of it from her.

Ashar waited until he was in the safety of his room, where he was the only person who inhabited the space. He felt incredibly lucky when he first found out, but Savar had glared at him and told him that his not having a roommate could change at a moment's notice. But, in the meantime, Ashar had been enjoying every moment of his alone time. Even if he would sometimes lie awake wondering what kind of things Kareem and Ovi were discussing in their rooms.

Who cares? he told himself, staring at the back of his closed bedroom door and allowing himself to focus. After a quick *whomp-whomping* sound in his brain and a swish through the air, he knew the portal had been created, and he opened his bedroom door. Instead of stepping into the halls of the House of the Venari, he stepped out of some sort of shop and spilled onto the sidewalk of a very busy street. A bit disoriented and also in awe, he turned to see which shop's exit he'd just used as his portal. He stepped backward to admire the elegant formalwear storefront, unknowingly *right* into the road, where he was nearly struck by a taxicab. A horn blared, and he swiftly jumped out of the way, narrowly avoiding them. He stood on the sidewalk, taking a moment to catch his breath, staring at his surroundings. One look at a double-decker bus and Ashar knew he must be in London. He hadn't thought of this place specifically; he had just been concentrating on finding somewhere he could get some birthday supplies for his uncle.

The street he was on now was particularly busy, the road flanked by rows of tall buildings adorned with brick facades and neatly aligned windows. Along the sidewalks, pedestrians bustled about, some hurrying along with determined strides while others meandered leisurely, tourists taking in the sights. Traffic in front of him built quickly because of the taxi's sudden halt to avoid hitting him. Cars inched forward, the drivers in them looking agitated and honking their horns. A bus up ahead stopped to pick up and drop off more passengers. People on bicycles darted in and out of the lanes almost recklessly, but something told Ashar that they just had a lot of practice bicycling in a city like this.

Ashar smiled as he started walking. He loved this bit. When it came to his gift, he often thought of himself as the luckiest guy in the world. But then, sometimes, he felt the opposite. It depended on the situations he was put in. But he loved the human world. He loved their way of life. How different cultures were from city to city. He loved people-watching. He loved sightseeing. He loved trying different foods, not because he was hungry but because they simply smelled too good to resist. Like now, as a fruit vendor nearby called out to him, the scent of freshly baked bread wafted through his nostrils from the bakery he was strolling past.

Ashar waited until the produce guy was distracted with other customers before he nicked one of the apples and carried on with his business, biting into the delicious fruit and reading all the store names until he found one he wanted. Squeezing past a couple of tourists who were crowded behind an unfolded map, talking to each other in stressed-out voices, Ashar entered a market that had *just* what he needed. He spotted the objects straight away: a birthday cake in plastic casing, ready to be cut and served; behind it, along with the other cakes, was a massive selection of pre-filled helium balloons. He browsed the rest of the store, waiting for the perfect opportunity. And when he was certain the coast was clear, he picked up the cake and a handful of birthday balloons in an assortment of colors. Then, he dipped into the back hallway that was meant for employees only. He heard somebody call out, but he couldn't be certain if it was to him. Before he could check, he was already opening a door and stuffing through back into his bedroom at the House of the Venari.

He hardly ever got caught stealing *before* he got his gift, but now, it was just too easy. Still, a familiar sense of guilt washed over him. He was tired of having to resort to theft. He knew it was wrong. But he promised himself a long time ago that as soon as he completed Venari training and finally had the money, he would go back and pay for everything he had stolen before.

When classes were done for the day and Ashar was finally caught up on all of his schoolwork, he teleported straight to his neighborhood in southern Rhapta. He hurried down the baobab-lined boulevard to his house, realizing he was a bit later than he should be. In this part of Rhapta, things were a bit more chaotic. So many people had moved here from the outskirts in such a short period of time there was hardly any time to check that there was room for everyone. It resulted in everyone being packed in a little tighter. And instead of single-family homes, there were multiples stacked together side-by-side and story by story, connected by a winding stone staircase.

Ashar stopped in front of a courtyard encased on three sides with three separate houses, three more on top of those houses, and one winding staircase in the center of the first main building. He walked behind the staircase, his house on the ground floor, shaking his head at the disaster that was the courtyard. Weeds were well overgrown. Trash was littered about by all the other families. Yet amid the mess were children's belongings—a faded ball here, a well-loved jump rope there. Kids' toys were the only mess he enjoyed seeing. And near the staircase lay one that caught Ashar's attention every time: Rhaptan puzzle stones. He had loved those as a kid. The flat, smooth stones were collected from the riverbanks around the city, and each stone was carefully painted by local artisans with vibrant colors to depict various animals found in the nearby wilderness. Ashar was certain these belonged to the adorable little girl who lived next door. She loved to be outside. Ashar didn't blame her. He was that way, too.

He stepped inside his minuscule home, appreciative of it despite always wishing for something greater. The smell of delicious food wafted through his nostrils, and he froze in the entryway at the sound of a familiar voice. A feminine one. Definitely not his uncle Adil.

Nasrin, he whispered. His stomach flip-flopped. His pulse quickened. He heard her laugh somewhere in the house, and he heard the quiet sound of Adil's joining hers. Ashar didn't know she'd be here. But he should have known. Of *course* Nasrin wouldn't want to miss his uncle's birthday. Nasrin was around so often that she was basically part of the family. And he was sort of part of hers.

Starting the party without me? Ashar asked, walking down the narrow hallway through the kitchen and into the living area, where his uncle sat on a dingy cushioned chair while Nasrin stood behind him, giving his hair a trim.

There he is, Adil said warmly.

Nasrin paused her trimming and turned around, looking at Ashar with her amber-brown eyes. It nearly knocked all the breath out of him. He didn't understand it. He saw Nasrin all the time. He'd known her since they were little kids. He didn't used to feel this way when seeing her. He wasn't even sure when it started to change. But now, it happened every time he saw her. It even happened every time he *thought* about her. At least lately.

Nasrin's eyes sparkled gold, her lashes thick with natural volume. Her high cheekbones had a pretty blush on them, and the most stunning smile he'd ever seen filled her face.

There you are, she said, swatting him on the shoulder as he passed by with the balloons and cake to go around to the front of the chair and hug his uncle. *Took you long enough.*

What's this? Adil asked as he saw his balloons and cake.

Only the best for the best! Ashar said, leaning forward and hugging his uncle, not wanting him to get up. Adil's joints ached terribly these days. Ashar knew some exercise would probably do him some good, but it was his birthday, so all Ashar wanted today was for his uncle to be comfortable.

Which exciting town did you run off to this time? Nasrin asked, eyeing the colorful balloons. Initially, Ashar hadn't told Nasrin about his gift. He only got it a few years ago after thinking he was destined for a life without an ability. He worried about his freedom. He didn't want the Rhaptan government to find out what he could do and take it upon themselves to select Ashar's job and his future for him since it was an ability that was so powerful and valuable. Naturally, he couldn't keep the secret forever. Once he suspected he was being followed and watched, he decided to open up to Nasrin so she could offer him some guidance. She was the only one he trusted to tell. That, and he didn't want the news of his ability to get out and get told to Nasrin from someone else before he had the chance to—she'd never forgive him for that.

Just took a casual stroll through London, Ashar replied smugly. It drove Nasrin crazy that this was his gift. Ashar wasn't sure why, though. He could take Nasrin anywhere she wanted to go. All she had to do was ask. She might as well have had Ashar's gift herself.

Nasrin scrunched up her face at him, a look that was completely adorable to Ashar. *You could've brought me, you know.*

I went during my break at the House, Ashar explained. There wouldn't have been enough time to go grab her and get back to school on time for classes to resume. He didn't want to draw suspicion to himself either. Ashar wasn't completely sure how his ability got found out. His best guess was that someone noticed his frequent disappearances, tried following him only to find a door without him on the other side of it, and then reported it to a person of a higher position, who then assigned guards or other Rhaptan workers to keep a careful watch on him. One day, he was in Tokyo, singing karaoke, and then he came back to Rhapta and was escorted by guards right to the Grand Hall.

Nasrin rolled her eyes and resumed cutting Adil's hair. Even though a lot was cut off already, Ashar could tell how long it had gotten since he last saw him. Had it really been that long ago? By the looks of the length of his hair, it must've been months. Ashar tried to pop by more often, but the times he had over the past few months, his uncle hadn't been home. Ashar had only been able to leave a message for his uncle, along with some money and food on the counter. But he caught up with Nasrin about how his uncle was doing. She lived in the same courtyard, just upstairs and one over.

Ashar walked into the kitchen to set the cake down on the small table already set for the three of them. He hung back, watching his uncle and Nasrin hang out together. There was so much of the world to see. So much Ashar could do. So many places he could go. But at that moment, there was nowhere else he would rather be than right there. Living his own life instead of the life of the guy who spent time floating aimlessly through busy cities.

It was a wonderful evening. Ashar hadn't seen his uncle laugh so much in a long time, and it was because Nasrin and Ashar were particularly lively that night, bickering playfully with each other constantly and reminiscing about the things they did in their childhood together. But Ashar's favorite part was when his uncle started telling them stories of Ashar's parents. How Ashar's father was a bit of a ladies' man, but once his mother set her sights on him, there would be no giving up. She knew they belonged together, and she waited "with her arms crossed and her eyes rolling" for his father to finally figure it out. Without a doubt, it seemed Ashar's uncle knew that his parents would've been together for years and years if they were still alive. And while Ashar listened to the story, he couldn't help sneaking glances at Nasrin, wondering what kind of thoughts went through her head about him. He wondered if she ever had thoughts like that. Ashar was kind of a ladies' man himself. What if Nasrin had the same idea as his mother had? What if she was silently waiting on the sidelines for him to realize that he was supposed to be with her?

There's no way, he told himself, shaking his head, eliciting a look from Nasrin that made him quickly look away, back to his uncle, who was in the middle of telling a story about a fight he and his brother—Ashar's father—got into over a girl when they were just toddlers.

Nasrin couldn't possibly think of me like that, could she? Ashar wondered. Was he completely one-sided in this? What if he was the only one who noticed that things seemed different between them?

IT WASN'T until late in the evening that Ashar and Nasrin finally told Adil that he needed to get to sleep, and he left just Nasrin and Ashar alone in the small kitchen together, cleaning up the mess they made.

Do you want to go sit by the fire? Nasrin asked as she dried her hands on a dishcloth, giving Ashar a kind smile.

Sounds great.

Ashar turned down the lanterns and lamps inside the house and walked out into the courtyard with Nasrin. Nasrin swiftly created a couple of swings for them out of strong, thick vines—as her plant-growing ability allowed her—in front of the fire pit, and Ashar got to work lighting the fire. They sat down on the swings, and Nasrin gently swayed in hers while Ashar found himself sitting very still.

So what's it like? she asked. *How's it been going?*

At the House?

Yes, silly.

He shrugged.

Come on, don't give me that, she said. *I've hardly heard from you. I assumed it must be going fantastic.*

You'd probably think so, Ashar said. *But remember, I'm not the one who wanted to do this in the first place.*

Trust me, I know. You still haven't come around? Nasrin was the one who really pushed Ashar to become a Venari. Ashar didn't know how he felt about it. When the Rhaptan government found out what he could do, Ashar had to endure several meetings and lots of talks about what they were going to do with him because, *just* as Ashar suspected they'd think, the government decided a gift like Ashar's simply could *not* be wasted. Eventually, Zaid talked to him, telling him about how he should become a Venari. This would be the best way to ensure his usefulness to the government while also letting him have the freedom to travel all over the world. When Ashar explained the talk he had with Zaid to Nasrin, she was completely on board. His uncle was proud of him, too.

But Ashar did miss his freedom. He never saw himself being a Venari. He always saw himself as a street rat. And then when he got his gift, he saw himself as a street rat with a very large map.

I don't know, Ashar said.

She smiled and shook her head, looking down at her feet.

What? Ashar asked, his curiosity piqued.

I was just thinking about the day you told me about your ability. Or should I say—the day you showed me. She softly laughed, and Ashar broke into a grin over the memory. He had Nasrin meet him in the courtyard, where he told her he wanted to show her something inside his house. Only, he had turned the front door of his home into a portal, and when they stepped through it, they were in the very first diner Ashar had ever teleported to. It had his favorite cherry pie, and Ashar decided Nasrin *needed* to try it.

You were like the living dead, Ashar teased, remembering how still and stiff Nasrin had been the entire time they sat at the booth inside the diner. It had taken her a while to process what Ashar had done. What he could do.

I still don't understand why you are so fixated on that dessert. It was far too sweet! Nasrin said.

Shall we go back right now so you can try it again?

Nasrin ignored the question and instead changed the subject. *I hope you're* actually *paying attention and getting all your Venari work done and not running off to various cities every night.*

Well, don't be too hopeful. Come on, Nas, you know I hate school.

But it's not like regular *school. This is much different! It's Venari training! You can't honestly tell me getting to learn how to fight and capture isn't at all exciting.*

Ashar shrugged and studied the twinkling sky above. *I guess the only thing that's okay about it is that my group and I sort of have our own secret mission going on in the background of things.*

What are you talking about? Nasrin demanded immediately, no longer swinging. Instead, her eyes narrowed at him, and she leaned a bit closer. This was her "protective sister" look. She and Ashar were the same age, but Nasrin used to say she was like an older sister to Ashar.

But that was then.

Would she still say that now?

I can't really say much, Ashar explained. *I don't want to put you in any danger.*

Danger? Ashar, are you in some sort of trouble?

No. But there's someone out there who is. Maybe multiple someones. And we're doing something about it. It feels good. To be doing something.

Did your teacher send you on the mission? Is it like an assignment for becoming a Venari?

Nothing like that. He picked a twig off the ground and chucked it into the fire. *Our teachers don't exactly know. At least, we hope not.*

I can't believe you, she lilted.

What? It's fine. Don't look so worried.

I'll look worried if I want to. Because that's exactly what I am. Worried. Are you going out into the field? Outside the barrier?

Nasrin, I really shouldn't say anything else about it. I promised my team.

Right. He watched her jaw clench. *You and your new friends.* Her tone was bitter.

Do I sense some jealousy?

What are you talking about?

Let me remind you that I wouldn't have this new group of "friends" if it weren't for you.

I'm not jealous, she snapped, getting to her feet. *I just don't like this. I thought becoming a Venari would be good for you. And for your uncle. I don't want you jeopardizing that. Almost as much as I don't want you to get hurt doing something stupid.*

He stood up next, stepping toward her. He tilted his head to the side and grew a wry smile on his face. *Aw, is Nazzy worried about me?*

He reached out a hand to tuck some of her minuscule braids behind her ear, but she swatted it away and turned around.

Shut up.

Don't be like that, he said with a chuckle. He'd spend all night getting that smile back on her face if he had to. Something told him it would be easy. Things always were with Nasrin.

But in the back of his mind, he was seeing things in a clearer picture now. He supposed he hadn't really thought too deeply about what he was getting himself into with Kareem and the others. But Nasrin was right. He needed to become a Venari, his uncle being the biggest reason why. What would happen if Ashar lost sight of his goals?

CHAPTER 10

ECHOES OF THE LOST

After Kareem grumbled and moaned for quite a long time once Ashar broke the news to the team that he wasn't going to attend their meeting, Kareem decided to just cancel it altogether. He was in a bad mood and figured if Ashar could mysteriously disappear without having to tell anyone where he went, maybe Kareem could do the same. He decided to tell the others he just remembered he had something going on anyway, and then he left the House of the Venari and walked through the bustling cobblestone streets of Rhapta. It had been a while since he had been home, and he figured it would be good to catch up with his family and check in on things. He wasn't sure how much they knew about the trouble he had been getting into at school. He knew that his older brother, Tejas, knew a lot, and he wondered how much his dear brother had told their parents. Or if his younger sister, Akilah, had heard the rumors and spread them like wildfire. It would be just like her to do so. Kareem was already annoyed at her just thinking about it, even though it hadn't actually happened yet.

The walk from the House to his home felt almost as though it had never happened—he had spent the entire duration of it deep in thought about Ashar and what he could be up to *now*. Kareem knew he agreed to trust him, but it was easier said than done. And how was Kareem supposed to keep up that act when Ashar went and behaved like he had earlier?

It wasn't as though Kareem was in the wealthiest part of Rhapta by any means, but he did consider his home to be one of the nicer ones. His family did pretty well in the city. With Tejas already a Venari himself, he was able to provide his family with a lot of income. Neither of his parents had overly fancy jobs, but they worked hard, and from what he understood, his father, Dumi, came from a family with a bit more money than many of the others and had inherited this money when his father—Kareem's grandfather—passed away many years ago.

Dumi took great pride in their front courtyard. It was immaculately kept. Neatly trimmed bushes, colorful flowers, and vines going up the side of the white limestone home. The panes of glass on the windows were sleek and shiny. The ornately carved front door looked glossy, as though it had just been polished. As Kareem stepped up onto the front porch, he couldn't spot a speck of dust. Not a single trail of dirt. He smiled at the sight of it, glad—and maybe just the *tiniest* bit disappointed—that his family seemed to be getting along well without him.

He opened the front door to a small entryway with a long hallway that led to the main part of the house and immediately called out in his head, *Mama? Father? It's me, Kareem.* Then, he waited for a response. None came. However, Kareem *did* notice the sound of people internally conversing somewhere in the house. There was a deep, throaty voice he didn't recognize and a feminine-sounding chuckle that did not belong to his mother.

Hello? Kareem called out again as he walked down the hall and turned the corner. Thankfully, his annoying little sister was nowhere to be seen in the kitchen or living area of their home, but there were two strangers sitting at a large rectangular table drinking some tea while Kareem's mother and father danced around the kitchen in synchrony, cooking up something that smelled delicious of guinea fowl eggs and beet bread and reminded him of home. Guinea fowl eggs and beet bread were one of his favorite meals.

Hello, the woman said, giving Kareem a pleasant nod. She had very short, tightly coiled hair, and her features were slightly sunken in as though she were sick or starving. At her greeting, all heads snapped to Kareem.

My son! his mother, Nyako, cried, putting a hand to her heart in surprise and beaming at him. She immediately started pointing her spatula at him in a scolding way. *Next time, don't wait so long to visit your mother.*

Kareem, what brings you home? his father asked.

Kareem was still curiously eyeing the strangers in the house as he answered his father. *Just thought I'd come home for a home-cooked meal for a change.* He cleared his throat. *Hello,* he told the strangers since his parents weren't introducing them. *I am their son, Kareem.*

Nice to meet you, Kareem, the shiny bald-headed man with a beard replied in that deep, throaty voice. *I am Agu, and this is my wife, Paki.*

Kareem looked to his mother, still wanting further explanation.

Kareem, darling, these are our new friends. We met them on Auraday. We had the best time with them. You have to hear some of their stories. Oh my heavens, your father and I could listen to their stories all day! His mother gave them both an adoring smile.

Kareem gave them a half-smile. *It's nice to meet you.*

Well, go sit, his mother said. *Sit and chat while we finish up dinner.*

Kareem did as instructed, although this wasn't exactly what he had pictured when he thought of going home for the night. He wasn't exactly in the best mood to be entertaining strangers. He didn't feel like he could fully relax and unwind and be himself as he hoped he could in his own home. He was always tense and on high alert, putting up a front at school, but here was supposed to be the haven where he could relax and be himself.

Your parents have told us much about you, Paki said. *That you are training to become a Venari. Is that correct?*

Kareem opened his mouth to reply, but then someone's voice coming from up their small, rounded staircase interrupted him before he could.

Did I hear Kareem down there? his little sister called down, followed by the noisy clamber of her footsteps as she hurried down to see him. *I heard you keep getting into trouble at the House!* Akilah stood with her hands on her hips as soon as she reached the last step of the staircase and had Kareem in her full sight.

Great, Kareem thought to himself.

Akilah, that is not a suitable topic to discuss when we have guests over, his mother said, thankfully coming to Kareem's aid for once. *Sit down, will you? Dinner is going to be ready soon.*

Kareem and Akilah sat at the table on the other side of Agu and Paki, and while Kareem's little sister continued to look at him as though she were dying to ask him a million more annoying questions about how things were going at the House, Paki, and Agu kept her busy by asking her questions. His sister didn't seem to mind too much. She always liked having the attention on herself.

Dinner was finally served, and his parents sat down at the table with them. The conversation stayed on the topic of his sister, what she was learning in school, and what she hoped her ability would be when and *if* she got one. Kareem got to mention a little bit about how his ability came about, but then the topic changed directions to Tejas, and suddenly, his parents couldn't stop raving and bragging about Kareem's older brother. All this talk about Kareem's siblings and so little talk about Kareem himself—Kareem tried to tell himself he should be glad that he didn't have to partici-pate in small talk, but still, the fact that he seemed to be ignored made him feel small and insignificant. It also made him worried that his parents were purposely keeping the topic of conversation off him because they were going to want to talk to him more about everything that had been going on at the House of the Venari, and in *private*, when their new fancy, funny friends weren't around.

Now, I forget, Kareem's father said after a while, aiming his fork at Agu, *did you tell me you had a kid? A son, right?*

Yes, remember, husband? Kareem's mother answered before Agu could. *He's just a few years older than Tejas.*

That's right, my father said with a nod. *What did you say he did for work again?*

The couple looked at each other for a moment, and then Agu looked down at his plate while Paki wiped her mouth with a napkin and straightened up in her seat. *Actually, our son is a Venari as well.*

Kareem's parents seemed to miss the looks on the different faces as they smiled gleefully with wide eyes. Kareem's stomach dipped. He didn't like the look on their faces. He had a feeling something was off.

That's wonderful! Our sons probably know each other then! Kareem's mother cried.

It's possible, Paki said slowly, placing a gentle hand on her husband's shoulder. *But our son... He's been gone. For a long time.*

Gone? Kareem's father asked. *What do you mean?*

Kareem already knew.

Paki looked uneasy about giving her answer. *He's one of the ones who... who went missing.*

That's terrible, Kareem's mother replied, setting her fork down as though she had lost all of her appetite.

It is. We... we've actually lost all hope that he'll ever come back, Paki said. *So we're just trying to accept it and learn how to move on. It's been a difficult process.*

I'm so sorry that happened to you, Kareem said, leaning forward as he stared at the couple with earnest eyes. Suddenly, a sort of realization slammed into him, and he felt like he was meant to come home to dinner that night. Like he was meant to meet these people and learn this story.

Slowly, Agu returned to his food, eating quietly while Paki smiled fondly at Kareem. *That is kind of you to say.*

They were silent for a long while, an awkwardness hanging in the air before his sister broke the tension. *The food is really good. Even better than last time!* She turned to Paki and Agu. *I've been craving this for weeks now. It's my favorite meal!*

Kareem had nearly forgotten Akilah was even there; she had been so strangely quiet. Akilah hadn't had many bad things happen in her life, so she didn't know how to cope with talking about such a heavy subject. Kareem almost couldn't blame her—except he was still curious about something.

Sorry, Kareem said to Paki and Agu, gently interrupting. *What was his name? Your son?*

He could feel his parents side-eyeing him like they didn't approve of him not being willing to change the subject when it was clear their guests were uncomfortable talking about their missing son. But Kareem was determined, so he ignored them.

Neelan, Paki said.

Kareem surely would've choked on his food had he taken a bite when she said it. Their son was *Neelan?* Neelan's *parents* were sitting at his family's table? He couldn't believe it. Pain squeezed his chest, and any bit of appetite he had completely left him in an instant. It was clear Neelan's parents loved him a great deal. It was clear they were suffering. And the fact they had lost all hope... it nearly crushed Kareem and broke him up into thousands of tiny pieces. If Kareem hadn't felt like he wasn't doing enough or acting quickly enough to figure out what happened to Neelan and find a way to bring him back, he certainly did now. This had to be a sign. Some kind of message. Kareem felt this very strongly. He heard the message loud and clear. He wasn't doing enough. He needed to try harder to get to Neelan.

Did you know him? Paki softly asked after a while of Kareem not saying anything. He quickly nodded his head.

I do, actually. Not well. I had only been at the House a short time before... it happened.

They talked about Neelan for a little while longer while Kareem and even his sister remained silent. Kareem tried his best to shovel down the rest of his now tasteless dinner, and then he abruptly got to his feet once more.

Oh, jamani! he said in a loud internal voice, not even caring if his acting was subpar. *I completely forgot about this assignment I have due in one of my classes tomorrow.*

Kareem couldn't say goodbye to Neelan's parents and get out the door quickly enough.

He felt awful. His body trembled with the guilt he harbored inside of him. As he headed back to the House, he couldn't stop thinking about Neelan's parents. He couldn't believe that they had lost hope. Neelan's parents. If they had lost hope, what did that mean, exactly? Was he supposed to give up hope, too? Was Neelan really dead?

CHAPTER II

THE SKIRMISH PLAN

Once again, on a particularly hot and humid morning, Kareem and Ovi left their room together and stepped down into the training ring before dawn, ready for their second-ever skirmish. They weren't the first ones to arrive, but they were by no means the last. The other remaining members of their team joined them shortly enough, and together, they all eyed their classmates and other Venari who liked to hang around the upper banisters to watch the skirmishes. Kareem was nervous. He could feel that he wasn't the only one. He could see it in many of his classmates' eyes or in their fidgety body language. He wanted to be excited, as he could tell many of his classmates also were. But this day was incredibly important, not just because these skirmishes were going to be what brought them one step closer to becoming official Venari—there was so much more at stake. Kareem's plan for his team had to go *just* right.

Just like last time, Hessa Darvish stood in the middle of the ring, her hood pulled up. Amol and Laban stood near her, waiting with their hands clasped behind their backs as everyone finished gathering.

When Kareem looked around the ring, he noticed it was different this time compared to last. In the first skirmish, there had been five colored flags tied around banister posts with matching stones in the sand. Each team represented a color, and they had to fight to be the last team standing with all five stones. Kareem and his team had been hoping it would be the same setup today, but they weren't foolish enough not to prepare for other scenarios.

Kareem's eyes watched as another team's mentor walked around and gave each team captain a black ribbon, getting to Kareem's team last and giving Kareem a stern nod. Kareem stared at the ribbon, wondering what the objective would be this time.

Then, finally, Hessa looked up at everyone with her stern expression and began speaking, *Good morning, pupils, and welcome to your second official skirmish.*

First, for some *of us,* Idris's voice muttered quietly. Kareem and Ashar looked over and saw Idris and Caden glaring at them. *You're going to get* crushed, Caden said to Ashar, smiling sinisterly. Kareem didn't feel threatened, though. Didn't Caden and Idris know that with a fifth person on Kareem's team, it was even *more* likely that Ashar was going to succeed? Or that he *would,* if that were his and the rest of the teams' actual goal that day.

Just ignore them, Kareem instructed Ashar. *And stick to the plan.*

Ashar nodded, and they returned their attention to Hessa.

You should all be settling in well to your new lives here at the House of the Venari, she continued. *You've been learning valuable lessons. You've improved your knowledge and your physical abilities—as well as your individual gifts—tremendously in a relatively short amount of time. We're excited to see all of that improvement play out today during this second skirmish. We look forward to seeing you put your skills to the test and see how you've bonded with your team over these past several weeks and grown with one another, learning to combine your efforts and create an unstoppable force.*

Kareem focused closely for a moment on each individual group, wondering just how well everyone got along. Wondering if any of them had truly found a way to combine their abilities and make themselves utterly and intensely elite. He had heard rumors about the team, with Idris and Caden not getting along so well. He hoped that was true. He didn't like the group much as it was, and on top of that, they were incredibly talented.

And as you all should know by now, I hope, Hessa continued, *it is not the same objective as the first skirmish. Nor is it the same objective as the preliminary test. This time, you'll notice each team captain holding a black ribbon. We want to see your abilities shine through this time, so we will not be allowing the use of the obsidian weapons or staves. The second your ribbon has been taken from your team and thrown down into the sand, or if you drop the ribbon and you do not catch it in time before it hits the sand, or if you unintentionally destroy your ribbon, your team is disqualified. The last team with one of your members still holding the ribbon will be declared the winner. And just like last time, the winners will be awarded an unsupervised assignment out in the field as well as two days off Venari training. Now, if none of you have any questions, please go with your team and find the spot you'd like to start in the ring.*

At once, everyone scrambled with their team to find a spot in the ring that was a safe distance away from everyone else. Kareem couldn't believe his luck. All he had to do was keep holding onto his ribbon? Was his gift of making things stick together really going to prove to be more useful than he had ever imagined before?

No, Kareem, he reminded himself. *That's not what the plan is. You cannot win today.*

He and his team members looked at each other and nodded. Tensions were high. Stakes were higher.

Kareem just had to stick the ribbon securely to himself, at least for a little while, until—

Begin! Hessa's voice announced the start of the skirmish unexpectedly, just like she liked.

Kareem panicked for a moment as everyone broke out into a run, lunging at one another, trying to get those black ribbons into the sand. He hurried to stick his ribbon to himself and then did a jump and rolled out of the way as Caden moved to slam into him.

Last skirmish, it was Ovi and Zara on defense. This time, the only one on his team playing defense was Kareem, as the others started around the ring to play offense and show off not only to their teachers but also to Zaid, Savar, and the others.

Even though the majority of Kareem's team didn't like to use their abilities, Kareem could tell they were a force to be reckoned with. All of their training had definitely paid off. They were much more in sync with one another and much more confident in their combat abilities, even without weapons. Instead of feeling desperate and angry, Kareem felt levelheaded and focused as he dodged various attacks from other classmates while also calling out advice and warnings to his teammates as everyone scrambled around the ring.

Kareem felt confident, strong, and also proud of his team. He was grateful for his gift because he knew his ribbon wouldn't accidentally fall from him; it would only hit the sand if it was ripped away, so he didn't have to concentrate on not dropping it like the other ribbon holders did. All he had to do was dodge attacks. He had been training to do just that for months.

He kept a close eye on Zara as she whipped her braids around and ran after Veer with his ribbon tied tightly around his wrist. Zara and Veer were both quick runners, but Zara caught up and lunged at Veer, knocking them both to the ground. They rolled around in the sand as Zara yelled in frustration at not being able to hold Veer down and get the ribbon off.

"Zara, pin him!" Kareem shouted as he caught a leg being kicked at him, twisted it in his hands, made Tarun fall to the ground, and then made Tarun's boot stick to the banister behind them.

Kareem looked back at Zara, glad to see she had managed to get on top of Veer and had a good hold on him with her body so she could use her hands to focus on getting that ribbon untied from Veer's wrist. But then, out of nowhere, Inaam showed up and gave Zara a swift kick in the side, sending her flying off Veer. She took over what Zara had been working on with Veer as if she wanted to get the ribbon away from him herself, even though it made no sense; it wasn't like the other teams got points for every ribbon they knocked to the sand. They just needed to be the last ones standing with their own.

Suddenly, the air around Kareem dried up so much that it seemed all the moisture had been sucked out of it. He gasped for breath and couldn't. There was no oxygen. And it was hot. So, *so* hot. At first, he didn't understand what was happening, but then he looked around and realized everyone seemed to be struggling as well.

Zara, on the other hand, was fuming as she got back to her feet and glared at Inaam, who had successfully gotten the ribbon off Veer and thrown it into the sand.

It can't be, Kareem thought to himself, staring at Zara in stunned shock. *She* was doing this. She was controlling the air and temperature around them—even if she didn't realize it.

When Zara finally tore her eyes away from Inaam, who was supposed to be her friend, she looked around at everybody else and finally seemed to realize what she was causing to happen. And then suddenly, Kareem could breathe again.

Yeah, Ashar! Ovi's voice cheered along with some others up above the ring as Ashar successfully tossed someone's ribbon into the ground and stomped on it with his boot. Kareem hadn't even been able to see how he had done it. He'd been too focused on Zara, who stood off to the side, momentarily not chasing after anyone, her eyes wide and her forehead bunched up in worry.

The skirmish went on, and it didn't take long for the exhaustion from constantly running and dodging other classmates to start wearing down Kareem. But he and his team were still managing to hold their own. Binita managed to fool one of the teams by changing into their captain's head and barking an order for them to hand the ribbon to her. Kareem also managed to watch as Ovi took a glove off his hand and held it up in front of Ekon, who was known to be wary of Ovi and scared of what secret, powerful hidden ability he had. The sight of Ovi's bare hand held up sent Ekon skidding to such an abrupt halt that he fell straight into the sand, face first, and Ovi plucked the ribbon from his grasp and dropped it to the sand with a satisfied smile.

Eventually, there were two teams left: Kareem's and Idris's. That meant it was time. That meant everything had gone accordingly, and it was more important than ever that this next part did so as well.

Kareem had to play it just right. He was the one who had to be the fall guy. Ashar, Zara, Ovi, and Binita distracted the team's remaining members, Idris and Caden—Inaam accidentally stepped out of the ring and was taken out—leaving just Faiza to go after Kareem. Faiza happened to be the one on her team carrying their ribbon as well, so Kareem knew he couldn't just run from her and not try to fight back. He decided the best course of action was to be so quick about his next move that it would almost be hard for anyone to understand how it went down.

Kareem ran from Faiza all the way to the edge of the ring. The girl with the weight of one of those clunky automotive things Kareem had seen out on the field was right on his tail. Kareem turned back to her abruptly and made the move like he wanted to —he slid feet first into her as though maybe he hoped to send her flying over him instead of landing directly on top of him. Naturally, it wasn't going to work like that.

Kareem cried out even *before* Faiza's small yet heavy body landed on top of him because he knew to expect the pain.

And it definitely came.

Bones in his body crunched, and Kareem's scream turned into a roar of pure agony. It had happened so fast that Faiza didn't even seem to know what had happened, and she quickly rolled off Kareem and looked at him for a moment as he yelled and rolled around in the sand, everything in his body hurting. He squeezed his eyes shut tight, and he felt the ribbon get pulled right from his shoulder where he had secured it. The pain had become so intense that his vision began to blur, and for a few moments, everything faded. And when he opened his eyes again, multiple bodies were running straight for him while somewhere in the background, people cheered victoriously for the winning team.

I was trying to—maneuver underneath her, he gasped out to Hessa, who dropped down beside him to check his injuries.

Was that *what you were trying to do?* she asked breathlessly before calling over her shoulder, *we need some healers over here!*

But healers were the *last* thing Kareem wanted, even if it sounded really good to him to not be in so much pain right then.

No, no, he cried out, opening his eyes again and seeing his teammates, as well as some other classmates, standing around him with worried expressions while Idris's team—the winners—continued to cheer loudly in an annoying, boastful way. Why did it have to be *their* team that won? *I don't need healing.*

Yeah, we got him, Ashar said to Hessa, reaching out a hand that Kareem took and allowed himself to be pulled to his feet, even though everything in his body screamed in protest. Ovi was quick to help, too. Zara stood right in front of Kareem and grabbed the front of his shirt.

Kareem, look at me, she said in a worried-sounding voice. He opened his eyes again and saw genuine fear in hers. *Are you* sure *you don't need healers?*

No, Kareem wasn't sure. He hadn't intended for Faiza's *entire* body to fall on top of his. He thought maybe he'd get his leg crushed, or his arm, or his shoulder. But it didn't matter how much pain he was in; Neelan could be somewhere at that very moment much worse off than Kareem currently was.

I'm sure, Kareem managed to say. *I... I'll be fine.*

I'm not even sure how you're standing right now, but if you say so, Hessa said, signaling to prevent the healers from approaching Kareem. She put a stern hand on his shoulder. *Wait here for me.* Then she jogged off to announce the winners and talk to them about how they were to be rewarded.

Once the commotion died down, Kareem and his team found themselves being approached not only by Hessa again but by Zaid and Savar as well.

Kareem's team. Although there is no prize for second place, you all did incredibly well today, and you should feel proud of yourselves, Zaid said with intensity.

Kareem, I really thought you had the potential to win it all again today, Hessa said. *I was astonished by your brazen move to try and catch Faiza off guard like that.*

It was stupid of me, Kareem said weakly. The pain was still so intense that he was dizzy, even being held up by Ovi and Ashar. *I was getting to the edge of the ring, and I had to do* something.

Let's hope you don't try such a foolish maneuver on an ubir out in the field, Savar added with a glare, *should you ever get the chance to go on an assignment in the future.*

I guess I just need to prepare a little better for next time, Kareem tried, his adrenaline spiking and taking away a tiny bit of his pain. Were the adults onto them? Could they tell that Kareem's team lost the match on purpose?

Kareem suddenly felt a pair of eyes on him that didn't come from the adults, and when he turned around, he saw Faiza standing in the distance with her team. She was eyeing him curiously while the others laughed and hugged each other and pumped triumphant fists into the air.

In any case, Zaid continued, *aside from Binita's head hopping and you sticking the ribbon to yourself, Kareem, and whatever that was, Zara—your team managed to get incredibly far without any of you truly using your abilities to their full potential. It's impressive, but it also shows us that you need more training with your individual abilities. So that should be your next focus during your training sessions building up to the next skirmish. Understood?*

Yes, sir, they replied in unison.

Savar raised an eyebrow at Ashar but said nothing, although he looked like he wanted to.

Kareem, if you're not going to take any professional healing, then I want you at least to rest, Hessa stated. *You look positively dead on your feet.* She looked at his teammates. *You will all escort him back there safely, won't you?*

Kareem couldn't believe it. For once, one of their plans had gone the way they wanted it to. For once, he, Ovi, Binita, Zara, and Ashar had really been a team.

CHAPTER 12

THROUGH THE PORTAL

Ashar had surprised himself by having a genuinely good time during the skirmish. He hadn't thought he would enjoy it so much. He hadn't thought he would be so desperate to get a ribbon away from somebody, and he hadn't had any idea how satisfied he would be to watch that ribbon fall into the sand—the boot stomp he had done on top of it had been for added effect. Something he hadn't been able to help but do.

Ashar wished his first-ever skirmish had lasted longer. He realized he had been silly that whole time, worrying since there was no way for him to use his ability during the skirmish—nor would he want to risk exposing what he could do to everybody—that he wouldn't be able to hold his own against everyone else with their abilities. He hadn't needed to be so concerned. All of his previous time spent dodging the guards and shopkeepers around Rhapta, who chased after him once he stole things to provide for his small family, had really paid off. Maybe he also had a bit of an upper hand because he was older than the vast majority of the trainees at the House; he had a bigger build as well as more life experience.

As Ashar and Ovi both helped Kareem make it back to his room, the team talked in excited whispers about how successful they had been at the skirmish. Even though they hadn't won, they were incredibly proud of themselves because not winning was exactly what they had been hoping to do.

As they all discussed it, it was clear to Ashar that the others agreed with him: the skirmish had been even more exciting than they all thought because, despite their loss, their team undoubtedly stood out among the crowd. And although Ashar didn't admit this part to them, it felt good to be a part of something—that was another thing Ashar hadn't expected to feel.

I'm so glad we were able to call the healers off, Binita said, walking beside Ovi and craning her neck to get a look at Kareem, wincing at the sight of him. *Even though I'm sorry that you are in so much pain, Kareem.*

With a clenched jaw and his eyes still squeezed tight, Kareem barely nodded at her.

Ashar looked over his shoulder to make sure they weren't being followed or watched by other adults. *I can't get over how incredible that was,* he told the others. *Eish, what a rush!*

Beside Ashar, Zara smiled, but only for a fleeting moment before she was back to looking worried about something. And her eyes kept glancing at Kareem.

It's going to be okay, Ashar quietly told her, nudging her playfully with the free hand that wasn't still helping Kareem to his room.

What are you talking about? Zara asked quickly, tossing some hair over her shoulder. *I didn't even say anything.*

I just thought you could use the reassurance.

I don't need it. Zara crossed her arms. *I know Kareem will be fine.*

They made it to Kareem and Ovi's room and helped Kareem inside and onto his bed, where he grunted out in pain.

Just remember, you'll feel better in no time, Ovi said to him. *Thanks for taking one for the team.*

Kareem nodded. Sweat drenched his body, likely because he was still in so much pain. He rolled away from everyone and faced the wall, curling up into a ball and keeping his eyes closed.

What's next? Ashar asked the others.

Let's just keep an eye on him, Zara replied. *I expect he's going to get checked on, so we're not going to be able to leave until the morning.*

So, the team hung out on Ovi's side of the room, trying to be quiet and let Kareem get his rest while they reviewed their plans for going to California via teleportation the next morning.

Just as they had predicted, it wasn't long before a teacher stopped by Kareem and Ovi's room to check in on how Kareem was doing. A short while after that, one of the healers also popped in to make sure their services weren't needed. And even Savar ended up showing up, though much later in the evening. He claimed to want to be absolutely sure that Kareem was going to be okay overnight once everyone else went to bed, but Ashar wondered if there was more to it—if Savar was making sure Kareem and his teammates hadn't pulled any stunts.

Eventually, Kareem somehow managed to fall asleep through his pain. Binita decided it was time for bed and that they needed a good night's rest before their big day. Ovi offered to walk her back, and Ashar decided he should head out, too. He smiled and held out his hand to help Zara up from Ovi's desk chair.

Zara sat with her arms crossed, not looking at anyone except for Kareem. *You all go without me,* she said. *I'll let you and Ovi have your alone time, Binita. I... I'm just going to make sure this idiot doesn't die in his sleep.*

Oh, uh... Binita batted her eyes furiously and glanced at Ovi, who looked equally uncomfortable. Ashar laughed at their awkward exchange, knowing that Binita and Ovi had feelings for each other but hadn't discussed them yet. It was amusing to Ashar to see Ovi and Binita getting so embarrassed about their not-so-secret feelings toward one another being addressed.

THE NEXT MORNING, Ashar arrived back at Kareem and Ovi's room, along with Binita, who brought some pastries from the dining hall, and Zara, who was yawning heavily and looked as though she hadn't gotten an adequate amount of sleep the night before. They were all dressed in their standard Venari training clothes—gray, loose-fitting attire that tightened slightly around the wrists and ankles to allow for easier movement—but underneath, they were supposed to be wearing their normal civilian clothing. In Rhapta, that meant bright colors and limited coverage because of the sweltering African sun. However, thanks to their human studies class and Ashar's teleporting experience, Kareem, Binita, and Zara had been versed in how to dress themselves to blend in a little better in a place like California. Ashar had told them to wear as many layers as possible because Northern California could get uncomfortably cold, and Rhapta didn't exactly make clothing like "*sweaters*" or " *tights.*"

All right, let's leave the Venari attire here, Ashar said, rubbing his hands together as he side-glanced at Kareem, who was sitting up in bed but still not completely healed. He didn't bother to hide his colorful, thin pants and gauzy shirt under his Venari lights since he hadn't left his room at all. Ashar knew it wasn't going to keep him warm enough this time of year, but he didn't care to point it out. *I already warned him once,* he thought to himself.

Ashar and the others shed their pupil uniforms and revealed their various colorful, patterned, layered outfits to one another. Ashar knew they'd still look painfully out of place in California, but it was better than all of them wearing the same light gray uniform.

Are you all ready to do this? Ashar asked, looking around at the others and stopping when his eyes landed on Kareem. He still didn't look well. *Kareem?*

Yes, Kareem said immediately, getting to his feet, although slowly.

Are you sure it wouldn't be better if you stayed here? Ashar asked him, genuinely just looking out for Kareem's best interest. Faiza had done a number on him the previous day.

There's not a chance that I'm staying behind, Kareem chided. *I am the team captain, remember?*

Ashar looked to Ovi, who shrugged. *Kareem should go. Besides, I really don't mind being the lookout. If anyone comes, I won't let them in the room. I'll say that Kareem needs his rest.*

Thanks, Ovi, Kareem told him.

Great, Binita said, chowing down on her pastry, bouncing up and down excitedly on Ovi's mattress. *So, let's do it then, Ashar. I can't wait to see your ability in action again. I find it fascinating.*

Ashar's smile faded a little at this. The thing was, he had the address of the SPE building, but he wasn't sure that it would help him appear exactly where he needed to in California. He'd never seen the building before. He'd never been to Northern California before, either. Southern California was where all the fun was. Northern California was colder and more forest-like. *Uh, yeah. Sure thing,* Ashar said, focusing on the door of Kareem and Ovi's bedroom and thinking hard about exactly where he wanted them to be the next time he opened it. *I need SPE's building to be on the other side of this door,* he thought to himself. He closed his eyes and concentrated deeply, all other noise fading away. When he opened his eyes, he found the others staring at him in anticipation.

Well? Zara asked. *Do you* have *to be the one to open the door?* She took a tentative step toward it.

Just in case, that might be better, Ashar said. He wasn't used to bringing anyone except Nasrin along with him when he teleported to different places, and now he was supposed to bring several others over with him.

Ashar stopped in front of Zara and opened the door. Just on the other side was the redwood forest. Gone was the musty hallway of the House of the Venari.

A cool breeze flooded Kareem and Ovi's room, and right through the doorway were the tallest and widest trees Ashar had ever seen. He looked back at the others, who had been stunned into total silence. *I guess we'll start here,* he said. He led the way, stepping in through the door. The others followed. While Ashar was certain they were in Northern California based on the massive tree trunks and their red bark, he knew they were in the wrong spot. The door they walked out of belonged to an abandoned shed in the middle of the woods. It looked like it used to accompany a house that had crumbled to nothing long ago.

There was no way SPE could be close to this. And with no signage, there was no way for the group to even know exactly what part of Northern California they were currently in.

This doesn't seem right, Binita commented. *But it sure is amazing.*

And freezing, Zara complained, rubbing her arms. She had on two shawls, but it wasn't enough.

Let's try again, Ashar said, closing the door to the shed they were standing outside of.

We're not going to be stuck out here forever, are we? Zara asked, looking around and shivering slightly. *I don't want to freeze to death. Why can't we be in the other part of California? The sunny part.*

I told you it'd be cold this time of year, Ashar reminded her.

Your commentary doesn't make me any less freezing right now.

I need to concentrate, Ashar told her. He tried again, focusing on the address and the SPE building he had seen a picture of.

He opened the door to the shed, and this time, things seemed more promising on the other side.

Hurry, Ashar said to the others, not wanting to draw attention to themselves in case anyone in the busy street noticed four people leaving an establishment whose interior through the doorway suddenly looked very different than it was supposed to.

They were in a small, busy downtown area, and the air smelled like saltwater. They were close to the ocean.

At least there are street signs this time, Kareem pointed out, leaning against the side of a brick building for support and eyeing the strangers who walked by with a suspicious gaze. Ashar wasn't sure why Kareem had this look; the passersby had a much better reason for their questioning, confused glances at them. Everyone was dressed in thick coats in darker colors that were more fit for their winter months. Ashar and the others looked ready to hit the beach on a hot summer day.

"Relax, would you?" Ashar asked out loud to Kareem. Kareem dropped his shoulders from under his ears in response, but he still looked miserable. Ashar figured he was just in a bad mood because he couldn't move very fast with his injuries still healing. He did look much better than he had the night before, at least.

Beside Ashar, Binita gasped. *Your voice!*

"We should all be speaking out loud when we're in the field," Ashar pointed out, "although quietly. We don't want anyone to hear our discussion, but we want them to see our mouths moving." It didn't feel weird to Ashar anymore to use his voice. But he was sure the others weren't going to like it too much.

Kareem cleared his throat. "Fine. Let's pull out the map and see how far away we are."

They all crowded around the unfolded map, trying to figure out exactly how to read it and determine where they were in relation to SPE's location. Ashar hoped that, to the locals, they just looked like silly tourists who hadn't done their research before taking a trip out there.

"This isn't going to work," Ashar said, shaking his head in frustration once they figured it out. They were still a good twelve miles away from their destination, and it would take them ages to walk there, especially with Kareem's slower-than-usual pace.

"What's going on, Ashar?" Kareem asked disdainfully, keeping his voice a low whisper. "Don't you know what you're doing?"

"You don't know how my ability works, okay?" Ashar barked out. "It's... complicated. It takes an immense amount of focus. And I'm not used to bringing this many people along. I've also never had a *true* desire to go to this place. It's a little harder to get the SPE building to be on the other side of a door than, say, my favorite diner."

"But who knows how long we have?" Kareem countered. "We don't know how long Ovi is going to be able to hold off on letting anyone check in on me. You don't understand how big of a risk we're taking doing this."

"Trust me, I do," Ashar said. "I'm part of your team, so if you all get kicked out of training, that means I do, too. And that's not something I'm willing to let happen. So just... shut up and let me concentrate."

Unfortunately, the third time wasn't the charm.

It took several more tries before Ashar finally determined that they were relatively close to the SPE building. According to the map, it was about a ten-minute walk, which was good enough for everybody else, even if Kareem had to drag along behind everyone. Ashar was fine with that, anyway. He didn't want to talk to Kareem at the moment. He needed some time to cool down.

That kid could be so annoying.

"I can't believe how much time has already passed," Binita commented as Ashar observed her looking down at her watch.

"That's Binita's nice way of saying we should probably go back soon before anyone gets suspicious." Zara continued to keep her arms crossed as they all followed the map, which took them out of civilization and back into a woodsy area. "Ovi doesn't exactly have a way of telling us if we've gotten caught or not."

Ashar could tell Zara was uncomfortable, and he wondered if it was because of where they were. "Are you *always* like this out in the field?" he asked her.

"You make it sound as though I'm out in the field *all* the time," Zara replied. "I'm not. I've only gone twice. And the last time, an ubir nearly chewed my arm right off."

This nearly caused Ashar to stop walking, but he didn't because he knew they were pressed for time. "Are you serious?"

"Dead serious," Zara replied. "I forgot—we never went into full detail with you of our last attempt to find Neelan."

Ashar swallowed.

"You're not too freaked out, now, are you?" Kareem asked Ashar from the back of the group.

"Not even a little bit," Ashar said coolly.

"I don't think I'll ever get used to hearing my voice out loud," Binita said out of the blue, moving her jaw around a lot. "This talking stuff is sort of a workout."

"Do you think there will be more ubir around the SPE building?" Ashar wondered aloud, ignoring Binita.

"I'd say it's possible," Kareem replied. "SPE knows what the ubir are. They're even working with them, giving them sacrifices for the blood rite in exchange for helping them locate Anunnaki."

"Cool."

While it also made Ashar nervous, the thought of fighting and capturing an ubir *did* sound intriguing. Multiple adults at the House of the Venari already knew what Ashar's ability was. If he went back and handed them over an ubir and claimed he accidentally came across it while on one of his many adventures, maybe they'd even count it as one of his unsupervised assignments. He could then be one step closer to graduating.

He had thought about this before, but he'd never teleported anywhere and come across an ubir, much to his disappointment.

At one point during their walk to the SPE building, Kareem suddenly dropped to the ground behind everyone. Ashar whirled around to him, Binita gasped, and Zara immediately dropped to her knees beside him in the damp earth.

"Kareem?" Zara asked, a hand on his shoulder. Kareem looked a bit off-color, but he didn't seem to be in pain. He just looked weak.

"I just need a second, that's all," Kareem muttered. He looked angry, as if he was mad at himself for not being stronger.

"It was a bad idea for you to come anyway," Zara huffed, still not removing her hand from him as she looked him over. "We don't even know the extent of the damage that Faiza caused; you could have twenty crushed bones your body's working to repair right now, Kareem. Not to mention, we didn't use more temporary ink like we should have." Before their last excursion outside of Rhapta, they'd nicked some of the temporary ink that would allow them to leave the city for a small amount of time without losing their abilities and memory after they tattooed themselves with it. Temporary ink used to be the only kind, and it used to only be available to Venari. Now, there was a permanent version as well.

"I didn't think we'd be here this long." Binita bit her lower lip. "I thought it was just a quick scouting expedition and that we wouldn't be gone long enough to start to feel the effects of not having the ink."

"I know," Zara told her. "I'm not blaming you, B. But without it, Kareem's not going to heal like he should."

Ashar wondered where they got their temporary ink from, but he didn't bother to ask. He had his own personal stash of it, given to him by Zaid—much to Savar's distaste—so that Ashar's teleportation adventures could be for as long as he wanted without the risk of him losing himself. Ashar's argument to get the ink was that no one was going to stop him from teleporting, so they might as well give him the temporary ink so that he didn't lose everything, disappear, and waste all the potential he provided the Rhaptan government with his ability. He was forbidden from sharing the ink with anyone else, of course. He didn't want to have to share it with his team in case Zaid or Savar decided to do an inspection of it and realized far more was missing than there should be.

Now, if only Ashar could get the new *permanent* ink and never have to worry about it again.

"Take as long as you need," Ashar said to Kareem. "We're almost there. We'll examine the place quickly, familiarize ourselves with it a little bit, and then we'll be more prepared when we come back next time."

"Stop trying to be so tough all the time," Zara said to Kareem, pushing him back to a seated position as he tried to get to his feet. "Listen to your body."

"My body's telling me to get this done so that I can get back and keep healing like I'm supposed to," Kareem argued.

Zara made him wait a few more minutes before she helped him back to his feet, and he accepted it begrudgingly. Then, they all walked at a slow pace with Kareem so that he didn't feel the need to push himself to keep up.

When they eventually made it to a sudden clearing in a dense patch of redwoods, Ashar's mouth fell open when he finally laid eyes on the commercial building, which was labeled as a specialty clinic but, from the exterior, looked more like a factory. All that was missing were the tall smoking chimneys.

"Some clinic," Kareem said with an eye roll. "Who would want to schedule an appointment for anything at a place out here like *this*? I mean, look at the road that leads to it!" He pointed to what had to be the world's bumpiest, narrowest unpaved road, which meandered around the building and disappeared from sight.

Ashar heard some clicking noises and turned to find Binita snapping several photos from different angles. The parking lot in front of the building was also unpaved, but there were no vehicles except for a nondescript white transit van. Ashar squinted. Maybe he was seeing things, but it looked like there used to be some sort of signage on the side of the van that had since been painted over—the SPE logo, perhaps?

"Binita, you better keep that phone super well hidden. We don't want it to fall into the wrong hands," Zara pointed out, shifting uneasily as if she wasn't sure it was a good idea for Binita to take photos in the first place.

"I didn't even know you brought a phone," Kareem said. "It probably would've been easier to use that for directions than the map."

Binita shook her head and put the phone away. "It's useless out here. No service. It only works with the 'internet.'" She put quotes around the word *internet* as if she thought it was some sort of mystifying unusual concept she didn't really understand the workings of.

"Okay, this is good," Ashar said with his hands on his hips as he took in the building ahead of them and its surroundings. "I don't want to get any closer in case they have a security system. I'm sure they already have an APB out on all of you from last time if the same people you dealt with before are the ones at this location now."

"It's hard to just stand here and not do anything," Kareem said. His jaw was clenched tight as he glared at the gleaming white building with fully tinted windows. "He could be in there. Waiting for help."

"And we're going to get him help," Zara reassured him. "We just need a plan."

This made Kareem scoff. "You're starting to sound like me."

"You should feel flattered." She rolled her eyes and turned away from him, and Ashar noticed the faintest of smiles tugging at her lips. Kareem stared at her for a moment without her realizing before he cleared his throat again and looked at Ashar.

"You'll be able to get us here quicker next time, right?"

"I'll be able to get us right through one of those doors." He nodded toward the building, which had a main front entrance as well as many side doors and fire escapes and a ladder on the side of the building going all the way up to the roof.

Ashar went on to explain to the others that they needed to find a different door to get back to Rhapta through because it was too risky to get near the SPE building just yet. So, after a small trek through the woods to another civilized area closer to the SPE site than where the team had last teleported, Ashar concentrated on the side door of a small pizza parlor, and when he opened it, he saw the interior of Kareem and Ovi's room, Ovi lounging on his bed with a book. He sat up immediately at the sound of the door opening, and everyone crowded inside, leaving California behind them.

How'd it go? Kareem and Ovi asked each other at the same time. They chuckled lightly.

Kareem sat down on his bed and slowly stretched out his limbs. *We found it,* he explained to Ovi.

Excellent, Ovi said with a grin. *No trouble here. You did have a couple of people try to visit you once. Waqas and Aryan. They wanted to check that you were okay and gush about what a good skirmish that was —nothing suspicious.*

Good, Kareem said, lying back on the bed and letting his eyes flutter closed. *When that next skirmish comes around, all I know is Faiza had better watch out for me.*

CHAPTER 13

MISSTEPS AND MISCALCULATIONS

Ovi found himself walking behind the rest of his group the following day at the House of the Venari. He kept finding himself lost in his own thoughts. The class had gone well, but Hessa Darvish had tried yet again to encourage Ovi to be open to the idea of seeing what his powers could do if he just tried to control them. The thing was, when it came to controlling his powers, Ovi wouldn't even know where to start. He only knew his gift had the potential to bring someone close to death or possibly worse. But he didn't like to even let thoughts of the latter cloud his mind. He pushed those as far back in his head as possible.

Do we really have to wait until classes get out? Zara asked, huffing as she walked beside Binita on the way to the dining hall for their midday break. *Why can't we just go now? We found—you know what —and it's time we got in there and got to Neelan.*

I know, trust me, Binita replied. *I feel the same as you. But Kareem is the leader, after all.*

He's infuriating, is what he is, Zara countered. Ovi knew Kareem could hear her because Kareem was closer to Zara than Ovi was, but Kareem had apparently chosen to ignore Zara's comments for once. Ovi supposed Kareem was a bit in his own head, too, because of everything with SPE and Neelan.

I don't think you mean that, Binita said to Zara.

Whatever. Fine. He... He does a decent job. Sometimes. Hardly ever. Right after Zara said it, she craned her neck to see if Kareem had heard her. Still, it seemed like Kareem's mind was not presently with them. Ovi wasn't sure if this made Zara more or less irritated as she scowled at him before turning back around to face the front.

Binita laughed at Zara's confusing attitude toward the team leader.

Throughout the midday break, Ovi found their entire group to be rather subdued. He wasn't even sure why they were all spending it together when it was apparent no one really had anything to say to one another. *So,* he stood, *I just remembered I have somewhere to be.* His eyes flashed to Binita for the briefest of moments before he nodded goodbye at the others and sauntered off.

Moments later, footsteps raced up behind Ovi, and then Binita was by his side. *To our hideout?* she guessed, a wide smile on her face. Ovi smiled back, glad he and Binita seemed to be so synchronized.

Inside the abandoned classroom of the science sector, Ovi and Binita made themselves comfortable behind Binita's fortress of stacked school desks. They stayed comfortably silent together, which Ovi didn't mind, but the reason he wanted to be alone with Binita in the first place was to actually be able to talk to her without the others listening in.

How are you feeling about later today? he asked Binita as she powered on the old computer, which whirred and buzzed loudly as it glowed to life.

A bit unprepared, honestly, Binita admitted. *And you?*

You're telling me—I haven't even been to California yet, let alone seen the location of those headquarters for myself. I'm definitely not prepared.

Binita huffed. Ovi leaned over and saw what she had loaded on the computer. Research. It looked as though Binita had been teaching herself more about the human world, specifically the American one. Ovi supposed she didn't think their humanities class was giving her adequate information. *Zara doesn't seem worried.*

Neither does Kareem, Ovi said.

I try to tell myself not to be. After all, we have gifts. Humans don't! It's just that... well, it's hard because I am not sure what to expect. And I don't like when I don't know what to expect.

ONCE CLASSES WERE FINISHED for the day, the five Venari in training met up inside Ashar's room, where he resided alone and, therefore, had less furniture taking up the place. Again, they had on their uniforms over the clothing they'd be wearing once they were back in California.

So, what is the plan this time? Zara asked. *Does Ovi have to stay behind again?*

Ovi decided to stay silent on the matter as he observed Ashar's bedroom. He wouldn't mind having to stay behind again, though he thought it might be a good idea for him to actually go. Ashar had collected all kinds of trinkets, presumably from all over the world. He didn't know what most of it was. There was something that looked like a small city inside of a clear glass ball. A small white ball with red stitching—Ovi thought maybe he had seen this one before. An American sports ball, though he wasn't sure which sport. Pinned up on the wall over his headboard, Ashar had a large map with colorful pushpins dotted across it. Ovi assumed they were all the places Ashar had been so far. And even though Ovi had never considered himself one who liked traveling, he was jealous to see how far Ashar had gone. How much knowledge he must have gained while seeing the world. Learning from what's happening around him, not just inside a stuffy old classroom. *No wonder Ashar does not care to be here,* he thought to himself.

I think we might want Ovi with us, should we need his abilities in an emergency, Kareem decided, shrugging at Ovi with a wince. *Sorry, O.*

No worries, Ovi replied, turning from the wall and nodding his head at Kareem. *I understand what you mean. In the right circumstances, sometimes there is no other choice. And saving any one of you is worth pulling the gloves off.*

You mean we might see your abilities in action? Ashar grinned. *Awesome.*

Don't forget—that's only worst-case scenario, Zara added. *We are hoping it doesn't get that bad when we are there. We want to infiltrate the place, figure out exactly what it is they're doing, and if they have Neelan. Maybe other missing Anunnaki, too. Then we want to get out of there totally unseen if we can help it. And that's where you come in, Ashar.*

Yes. Right, Ashar said, grabbing the back of his neck and looking away from everyone.

And you're sure no one followed us? Kareem asked Zara and Binita, who had been the last two to get to Ashar's room.

I only checked over my shoulder every few seconds, Zara said, bugging her eyes out at Kareem as though he should know better than to ever have to ask.

Okay then. Let's do it, Kareem clapped his hands together and then held them out to Ashar, letting him have the floor. *Ashar, you have the honors.*

Ashar let out a short laugh. *Well, hang on a sec.*

What is the problem? Kareem asked.

Ashar looked around at the others as though he wanted them to back him up. *We haven't even exactly made a plan for when we are inside!*

Kareem waved him off. *Yes, we have—it's to get Neelan!*

Zara inspected her nail beds. *I'm with Kareem on this—for once.*

But that is not nearly good enough. Come on, Kareem. I am co-team captain, aren't I?

Are you? Kareem asked, bunching his eyebrows together. *I thought you made yourself my "second-hand man?"*

Ashar blew air out his nose. *Just—here.* He stood in front of his bedroom door, and Ovi and the others waited as Ashar worked his ability and the air around them whirred with magic. After a few moments of standing absolutely still, Ashar relaxed, turned to smile at the others, and then opened the door.

The group stepped out of Ashar's room and into a very small, crowded hallway of a commercial building with black-and-white tiled flooring, a mop in its bucket tucked into the corner, and a door marking MANAGER'S OFFICE directly across from them.

Ashar led the way down the hallway, and Ovi discovered they were in some sort of eating establishment. The place was lively with humans, filled with the sounds of chatter and clinking dishes. Red vinyl booths lined the walls, and round stools with shiny metal bases lined a long counter. Women in slightly silly-looking uniforms moved quickly, carrying plates and refilling mugs. Some sort of machine in the far corner played music Ovi had never heard before, and the walls were covered with black-and-white photos and old memorabilia. It was so loud that Ovi almost wanted to cover his ears. He wasn't used to hearing so many people talk out loud at the same time in such a small space.

What in heavens is this place? Kareem asked, sounding half-irritated and half-amazed.

It smells… good, Binita pointed out, making the others breathe in deeply in reaction. She was right. The air smelled of greasy fried meats and sugary treats.

It's so cute! Zara gushed, her eyes sparkling as she looked around before she shot Ashar a grin. *I think I saw a picture of this in one of our textbooks.*

Probably, Ashar answered, leading them to a long, empty booth and sliding inside. The others followed suit. *They're famous in America. It's called a "diner."*

Diner, Ovi repeated, so enthralled, so curious, that he wasn't sure where to look next.

Okay, but why are we here? Kareem asked Ashar, the only one who didn't look happy to be there.

Are we close to SPE headquarters? Binita asked next.

Ashar flagged down one of the women in the weird outfits. *We're here to have some pie and come up with a plan.*

Pie? Zara asked, making a face of musing.

Don't forget—use your speaking voices, Ashar instructed. When the woman approached the table, she smiled big and put a red-manicured hand on her hip.

"What's up, kid?"

Ashar cleared his throat. "Lolita, I think this time, just bring us a whole cherry pie. Would that be all right? I don't doubt that between the five of us, we won't finish the entire thing."

The woman named Lolita shook her head and rolled her eyes. "You and your cherry pie, Ashar."

Ashar merely beamed at her, and Lolita walked off.

"She knows you?" Kareem asked Ashar with big eyes, using his actual voice. "On a personal level?"

"I'm what's called a 'regular' here," Ashar explained with a casual shrug as he slung his arm along the top of the booth behind

Zara's head. Ovi watched Kareem's reaction to this—Kareem sat up straighter and busied himself reading one of the signs on the wall, but it was still rather plain to Ovi that Kareem didn't like Ashar and Zara's closeness.

The pie arrived a couple of minutes later, and Ashar dished them all out a slice. "Doesn't matter if you have a need for food right now or not. This stuff is *worth* eating."

Everyone dug in at once, falling silent as they chewed.

"Um, wow," Binita eventually gasped, the first one to express interest in the dessert.

"This is... incredible," Ovi chimed in, wishing he could have at least three more slices without feeling too full.

"It's all right," Kareem muttered.

"A bit too sweet if you ask me," Zara added, meeting Kareem's eye.

"Because you're already sweet enough!" Ashar told her. Kareem went from looking moderately hopeful at Zara back to scowling in an instant.

"Okay—enough with the flirtation," he told Ashar. "What's the plan then, oh grand master of plan-making?"

"No, no, please, *you* go. I merely *stated* we needed a plan. Not that *I* could make one."

"What! You—you're insufferably irritating, Ashar, you know that?

"We don't exactly have any idea what to expect," Zara said. "It'll be hard to make a good enough plan when we don't know what awaits us inside."

"You know what else is good?" Ashar interjected, looking around the restaurant. "The cheese fries!"

"No!" Kareem barked. "That's it. We're leaving. *Now.* Ashar, throw down some American money and give us the door to SPE."

Ashar sank in his seat.

"What's the problem, Ashar?" Ovi decided to ask. It seemed to him there was a reason Ashar kept finding ways to keep them from getting where they needed to go.

"It's... my abilities. You guys don't get it. I—I don't know if I can just travel exactly to where Neelan is inside the building."

"Not even if you concentrate really, really hard?" Binita tried. Ashar gave her a sheepish wince.

"Okay," Zara said, sounding very levelheaded about the situation. "So we start on the outside and figure out a way to get in. I'm sure there's *some* way we can do it."

The team conversed for a while, and eventually, they came up with the best plan they could. Ashar opened his wallet and laid down some American money obtained over time from his previous travels, and then everyone followed him, their tummies full of delicious pie, back to the small, dimly lit hallway. Ovi realized the door they had arrived through at the diner belonged to the men's bathroom.

After a moment, Ashar pushed open the door to the men's room, and the teens all crammed inside, stepping out of a side door of the SPE headquarters.

"Well, at least we got past security," Zara pointed out, nodding in the direction of the gate at the edge of the parking lot, where two men in all white stood at their post. Once their door behind them closed, Ovi turned back to it. If only they could reopen it and find themselves inside the massive commercial building. When he tried the handle on the door, however, he found it to be locked.

It's probably fine to use our internal voices instead here, Ashar told the others.

All right, Kareem said, nodding at Zara. *Binita and Ovi will stay right here around the corner, okay? You go on in. Distract whoever is around, and then Ashar and I will sneak by and see what we can find. And don't forget the signal if something goes wrong.*

The signal being Zara simply yelling at the top of her lungs so the others could hear her and come to her rescue.

Zara swallowed. *Okay. But—I am taking Ovi with me.*

What? Ovi and the others said.

Last-minute decision! Binita, you'll be fine out here, won't you? Zara rounded the corner, and Ovi supposed he had no choice but to follow. It was easier than trying to tell Zara no. In any situation.

Ovi wasn't sure what he had been expecting when he pictured himself here at the SPE headquarters in person. He had known to expect the cold temperatures of Northern California, yes. He was dressed warmly enough for that. But the building stretched out before him as so huge. So intimidating. How big *was* SPE? What did they have in there?

Zara and Ovi entered through the double glass doors, finding themselves in a sterile, modernly furnished lobby. Ovi walked slowly behind Zara, who turned and shot him a sharp look as though to say, *keep up!* As she led them to the reception desk, where a woman in a black businesslike jacket and sleek, tight blonde ponytail gave them a scrutinizing stare. Sure, Zara and Ovi were dressed warmly, but they still didn't exactly blend in with everyone else in California. Ovi had known they wouldn't as soon as he saw those pictures of the locals on the computer at Binita's hideout earlier.

"I have an appointment," Zara announced to the woman, folding her hands on top of the tall desk and holding her head high. Ovi noticed she was even standing on her tiptoes, wanting to appear taller, apparently. SPE's headquarters fronted as a specialty wellness clinic. What sort of specialty services they offered, none of them could be sure.

I hope she knows what she's doing, Ovi thought to himself, his stomach knotting uncomfortably.

"Your name?" the woman asked with a raised eyebrow.

"Um, Eliza. Elizabeth. S-Smith."

"Okay…" The woman typed on her computer. "I don't see you on here."

"Well, that's not my problem, is it? Seems to me like you must have something wrong with your appointment system."

The woman eyed Ovi first and then went back to Zara. "How *old* are you guys?"

"None of your business!" Zara said to the woman, ignoring Ovi. "Who runs this place anyway? I *have* an appointment." She sounded more determined than ever. She was starting up the scene. Causing the commotion. "Look harder!"

The woman's eyes went back to the computer. "Uh, still nothing."

"Go get me someone else I can talk to. Your boss. *Someone*."

The woman squinted at her. "I'll… be right back, *miss*." She glared at them both and then disappeared behind a door.

Zara drummed her fingers impatiently on top of the desk, and she and Ovi pretended not to know or see Kareem and Ashar as they kept themselves ducked down and stormed inside the building, moving directly past Zara and Ovi without so much as a glance, and then they disappeared down a hallway.

"*Hello*?!" Zara called, leaning over the top of the desk,

What are you doing? Ovi complained. He didn't like this one bit.

I want to get as many people's attention on us as I can—lure everyone out here in the lobby and away from wherever Kareem and Ashar are exploring.

A couple of minutes went by, and no one had come back. The woman behind the desk was still gone.

"I don't like to be kept waiting like this!" Zara eventually called.

Zara, Ovi snapped, getting sweaty. *It's not working. I-I think something is wrong.*

Seconds later, the same door the woman at the desk had left

through reopened, and it was Ashar and Kareem who reemerged from it, escorted by two bulky, tall men in all white.

"You kids must be with them," one of the men said to Zara and Ovi. Ovi took them to be guards of the place. They were dressed the same as the men out in the busy parking lot in front of the gate.

"I-I have no idea what you mean!" Zara gasped, putting a hand to her heart. "How dare y—"

"Come on," the second guard demanded loudly. "All of you. Out. Now."

SILENT INTRUSION

It took all of the next day for Zara and the rest of the team to come to an agreement on when to go back to SPE to try again to find Neelan. This was their third attempt at sneaking off, and it was even more challenging because they had decided that breaking into the headquarters at night was their best chance of getting inside. In Rhapta, which was located in Tanzania, this meant they had to leave the House of the Venari bright and early, missing classes. Kareem announced the final decision on the rooftop before bed.

Zara hated the idea of skipping classes, but Ashar was all for it. He found them boring, except for combat training, and he was a bit of a rebel anyway. Binita seemed indifferent, while Ovi was mainly nervous about the potential repercussions, whether from missing classes or getting caught breaking into the highly secured SPE building that surely held their mentor.

They had to wake up that morning earlier than even the House's earliest risers to avoid being seen. Zara, who had been tossing and turning most of the night, worried about not creating a better distraction for Ashar and Kareem the previous night, found it easy to get up early. This time, they decided to meet on the rooftop, and once everyone was present, they climbed down the ladder and squeezed into the closet where Ashar first demonstrated his teleportation ability. Using that door, Ashar created a portal, and they stepped through directly into the dark lobby of SPE's fake clinic.

All was quiet. Zara noticed the locks on the glass doors through which she had entered a few days ago. It seemed no one was around.

"I guess this place doesn't have motion-detecting alarms," Ashar noted.

"Thank goodness for that," Binita chirped.

Zara was just relieved they didn't have to teleport outside for once; she hated Northern California's frosty weather at this time of year.

She looked around, considering their first move. She wasn't keen on splitting up in such a large building that was much too vast to be just a clinic. Hopefully, they would stick together, and they would find Neelan and perhaps even more.

There's an office door here, Ashar said, pointing to one behind the reception desk. *Should we start there?*

From what Ashar and I saw yesterday, the security to get to the deeper parts of this place is pretty tight. We might need a key or a passcode to get much further, Kareem added.

Then let's try it, Binita agreed, kneeling and pulling out a small, pocket-sized toolkit. As she worked on the lock, Zara glanced around nervously, half expecting guards to storm in at any moment. It was too quiet, and she wasn't sure she could trust it. Yet, she couldn't just suggest they abandon the mission entirely.

Hurry up, Binita, she whispered, her heart racing.

I'm trying, Binita muttered back, her fingers deftly working the lock. With a soft click, the door swung open, revealing a light and airy—though slightly messy—office, with papers strewn across the desk and books haphazardly stacked on slim, modern filing cabinets.

Zara scanned the room, her gaze landing on one of the file cabinets. *Maybe there's something in here*, she said, pulling open a drawer and rifling through the documents. Despite knowing many languages, whatever was written here was unfamiliar. The most she could decipher was the documents' detailed experiments and research, but they made little sense.

Anything good? Ashar asked from the other side of the office.

Zara shook her head bitterly.

We need to keep looking, Kareem urged, his eyes continuing to dart around the room.

Zara continued searching through the cabinet for documents that might make more sense. Behind her, she could hear Ashar shuffling through everything on the desk and inside its drawers.

Hey, what about this? his voice called out, drawing everyone's attention. Ashar held up a keycard, dangling it before them.

Zara stood. *Nice find. Let's see what it opens.*

The others nodded in agreement, and they all left the office, heading down the hallway Ashar and Kareem had explored a couple of days ago. Sure enough, they came to a distinct point in the eerie stillness where a door awaited them unlike the others. This one had a keypad on a stand beside it, and the door's material seemed to be made of some type of metal, unlike all the others, which had been wooden.

Zara examined the door. It looked reinforced and had a complex locking mechanism. *I have a feeling this is the one we want*, she said, excitement mingling with a surge of adrenaline and worry. It was a whirlwind of emotions to experience all at once.

Did it suddenly get really hot in here? Ovi asked, looking around at everyone.

Zara felt heat creep into her cheeks. *Sorry, that's probably me.* She hated it when her abilities got the better of her. She tried to calm her nerves as Ashar used the keycard on the keypad. The red light turned green, and following a few clicking and thudding sounds, the door slid open. On the other side was a wide metal staircase leading down into darkness.

Are we really *going to go down there?* Ovi asked, pulling the collar of his sweater away from his neck.

Don't worry. Zara watched as Binita grabbed his hand, but only for a moment before she seemed to remember how he hated being touched and quickly let go. *We'll all be together.*

Ovi nodded, and without further hesitation, they descended into the unknown.

The underground portion of the facility looked vastly different from the pleasant, airy upper floor. It was clear this part of the building wasn't public or known by many. The rooms underground were cold and dark, and everything was made of metal.

They wandered through the maze of enclosed and glass-cased rooms, their footsteps echoing ominously in the silence. As they looked through various logs and documents at different stations, they found records of more confusing experiments, along with equipment they couldn't identify and rooms filled with strange devices.

There's so much ground to cover, Zara pointed out.

Kareem nodded. *I think I know what that means. Time to split up.*

"Seriously?" Ovi groaned aloud. Even though the groan wasn't particularly loud, it felt amplified in the vast silence.

It'll be fine, Zara assured him. *Just remember the distress call.* She grabbed Binita's hand and pulled her along, and the group spread out.

I don't understand what SPE is doing in this place, Binita said as they started down a hallway with a dead end. The corridor led them deeper into the underground facility, the air growing colder and the surroundings becoming more sterile. They passed by several closed doors, each one labeled with cryptic symbols and numbers.

Other than stashing Neelan somewhere... Zara trailed off and stumbled upon an open room filled with cages. She and Binita stepped inside, and in the glowing lights of various computer screens, Zara noticed animals of all shapes and sizes in steel cages, their eyes wide with fear.

These poor little creatures, Binita cried out, immediately wandering away from Zara for a closer inspection of some of the cages to her right. Zara felt a surge of anger and sadness as well. How could they treat these creatures this way? They were living beings, not experiments.

Whoa. Zara, come here.

Zara turned away from a large, caged lizard and joined Binita's side. They were in front of a bizarre-looking container, one not like the others. It was made of tinted glass so dark she could hardly see inside. There was more than just a simple latch.

What's in there? Zara asked, her curiosity piqued.

Binita leaned in close and nearly pressed her face against the glass. *It's some kind of... creature,* she said, her voice filled with wonder.

Well obviously! Zara nudged Binita out of the way and took a look through the glass herself. Inside was a small, furry animal with bug-like eyes and soft fur. *It looks sort of like a weasel,* she commented, *but not a normal one.*

Yeah, I've never heard of a weasel with eyes that large, Binita agreed.

Zara stepped back. *It looks so...*

Cute! Binita finished. Immediately, she started fiddling with the strange latches. When she got the side of the case open, she slowly reached her hand in to touch the creature. Zara leaned in and watched closely as the thing nuzzled Binita's hand, emitting a soft purring sound.

I think it likes you, she said, unable to help the small smile on her face. It *was* pretty cute, after all.

He does, doesn't he? Binita agreed.

Zara raised an eyebrow. *He?*

With a quick glance around, as though to make sure no one was watching, Binita pulled the weasel thing out of the cage and cradled it in one arm, continuing to pet it with the other. It stared at her with its huge clear eyes and nuzzled closer to Binita, clearly loving every second of the attention. As Binita continued to stroke its fur gently with her hand, the creature began to glow, illuminating Binita and Zara in a mesmerizing sort of neon green light.

Zara gasped, taking a step back. *What is happening?* she whispered, her eyes wide with awe and horror. Her heart pounded with excitement and fear. She'd never seen anything like it! Where could it have come from?

Binita was just as much in awe of it. *Zara, it's... glowing!*

They almost didn't hear the footsteps growing nearer, and Binita hardly had time to hide the little creature within the confines of her shawl before Kareem raced into the room, looking a bit breathless. He looked like he had something important to tell them, but the words completely escaped him the moment he saw Binita trying to hide the glowing object in her arms.

What is that? he demanded, arching a brow.

Nothing, Binita tried.

Zara rolled her eyes. What would Kareem care about Binita finding the creature? *It's a glowing rat or something.*

Weasel, Binita corrected, giving Kareem a frown and revealing the animal to him.

What in the name of Rhapta...? Kareem trailed off, apparently at a loss for words. Then he shook his head. *That's not the weirdest thing in here.*

What do you mean? Zara asked, her stomach dipping.

Come on.

The two girls followed Kareem out of the animal room.

Kareem stopped and turned back to Binita. *What are you doing? You can't* keep *it!*

I know that! Binita cried. *I'm just... holding him. For now.*

How do you know it's a him?

That's what I said! Zara agreed.

Kareem let out a long breath and continued on his way, and the girls followed him to an office area where the desktop was covered in more files and papers.

What is all of this? Zara asked warily.

Records of the Anunnaki. Tons of them. Not of specific individuals but of us as a species in general. There are other names for us, too, but more or less, beings who have the same abilities and qualities.

That can't be good, Binita said in a small voice.

Kareem grabbed one of the papers and handed it to them. *Also —read this. It's a transcript. From... former Elder Tahir. And this person called the Director.* Tahir and his rebel groups had conspired to stop Kinza from becoming queen, and then after a monumental battle that destroyed much of Rhapta, Tahir and his loyalists lost the fight, and Tahir escaped. No one had heard from him since.

After reading it, seeing the way the former Elder Tahir revealed his powers, answered the Director's questions, and told him about Rhapta, as well as about the knowledge he obtained of its location, Zara suddenly understood things much clearer.

She turned to the others with a look of horror on her face. *So, the former Elder Tahir is how SPE came to find out about us in the first place?*

Looks like it, Kareem agreed.

No one knows what ever became of him, Binita said. *Do you think he's part of SPE now?*

I wouldn't be surprised, Kareem said, crossing his arms.

Just then, Ashar and Ovi rounded a corner and returned to them, looking like they had found something.

What else? Zara asked them.

A few of the records Ovi and I found looked like they might have referenced projects that sounded like the missing Anunnaki, Ashar explained.

*Most importantly—*Ovi removed a file from behind his back and held it out to them. Across it in big red letters was the word CLASSIFIED.

While Kareem snatched it and read it over, Zara looked at the other two boys. *What's in there?*

There's something in Peru, Ovi said.

Binita cocked her head to the side. *Something? What do you mean?*

The reports had a lot of redacted information. But it's pretty clear that it's something important, Ashar said. *Immensely important.*

What do you think it could be? Kareem asked, finally looking up from the file.

Well... there have been no signs of Neelan, Ovi pointed out. *No Anunnaki held in cages...*

Only animals, Binita pointed out.

That's when Ovi noticed the creature in Binita's arm. Since Binita had stopped petting it, it was no longer glowing. *Oh.* He stepped back as though uneasy.

Doesn't anyone else think this is a little strange? Zara decided to ask, looking around them again, all too aware of how quiet it seemed.

What? Kareem asked, meeting her eyes.

She put a thoughtful finger to her chin. *Just that no alarms have gone off yet.*

It was as though her words were what summoned it. Suddenly, all the lights in the facility went out, shrouding them in pitch-black darkness. There was a big bang. Zara screamed, and as her eyes adjusted, she looked up and saw a huge swarm of people in full tactical gear storming the room from multiple points of entry. Their guns were drawn. They were yelling. Their feet stomped loudly. Zara knew this had been too easy. She should have realized why—it was a trap. All along.

CHAPTER 15

THE NARROW ESCAPE

Thinking the others would move in the same direction as her, Binita ran for it. It didn't take long for her to realize she couldn't hear the footsteps of any of her friends behind her. She was all alone, fleeing from terrifying people; people who were running tests, conducting experiments, and locking up animals—and people!

No matter where she ran or how quiet she tried to be with her footsteps and breathing, it seemed like the team of SPE people remained on her tail. It was as though they could see in the dark! It wasn't the weasel still tucked into her arm that was alerting them because it hadn't started glowing again. She hoped it wouldn't start glowing anytime soon; she didn't need to draw any more attention to herself.

When she finally found a tucked-away corner where she thought she could maybe get away with hiding, she heard a manly voice yell out, "She has one of the specimens!"

Binita looked down at her bug-eyed friend. Still, he wasn't glowing. So how did they know? And what was she going to do? She thought her hiding spot was good enough, but it still seemed they knew not only where she was but also what she held with her. How could she let herself get backed into a corner like this? They were going to catch her. And who knew what was going to happen to her next?

Even though she had no idea how near they were, she had to take the risk. She jumped out of her corner and kept running blindly into the darkness. When a hand reached out and grabbed her arm, the one thankfully not holding the animal, she cried out, more terrified than possibly even when she had dealt with the ubir in Canada. They pulled her backward, and even though Binita expected something like a needle to be jabbed into her neck or her arms to be locked behind her back and put in handcuffs, none of that sort happened. Instead, she found herself being pulled into a room. Shoved, really. As quickly as the hand grabbed her arm, it pulled her sideways and then pushed her in. Then the door slammed closed.

A light from a lamp illuminated the space. Binita saw all the trinkets on the shelves on the walls. Somehow, Ashar had gotten his hands on her. He had been able to open up a portal while the men were chasing them and deposit her right inside this safe haven that was Ashar's bedroom.

Binita let out a cry of relief and sat there rocking on the floor, clutching herself and the weasel for a long while. When she finally calmed down, she let go of the animal, letting it explore the room. But it didn't want to go far. Instead, it was content on Binita's lap. So she stroked it once more, and again, her bug-eyed friend started to glow.

ASHAR KNEW these people had some sort of technology to help them see in the dark. That's how they were able to go in all the right directions even though everyone had split up when the rest of the team started running away from them. Ashar didn't have the special technology, but he did have visions in his head of all the doors he had explored while being in the facility so far. All he had to do was listen for the sound of his friends crying out, try to picture the area they were in, and then teleport from one door to the door nearest to them so that he could save them.

When he heard Zara's strangled cry as though someone had knocked the wind out of her, he opened a portal at lightning speed and was suddenly in front of her outside another door. He closed it swiftly, thought of the first room that came to mind inside the House of Venari, opened the door back up, and noticed the pressure in the air around them. The heat. He arrived just in time to see Zara clutch a man by the shoulder and give off a spark of shock. Although he was slightly afraid to touch her, Ashar pushed through the heaviness and grabbed Zara and also Ovi, who was wrestling with another guard and threatening to do something he did not want to do to him and threw them into what appeared to be the supply closet at the House of the Venari.

That was most of them. All he had left was Kareem, who wasn't one to cry out in fear as he ran from his pursuers. Ashar listened hard but couldn't hear his voice. At least, not until he heard someone else call, "Got him!" After that, he heard Kareem let out a scream of complete rage. Ashar was positive that Kareem was in the southwest corner of the underground facility. He opened the portal from the door nearest him and popped out behind all of the guards who were working hard to detain Kareem, who thrashed around wildly. Only three men had a hold on him. Everyone else still scattered about, trying to find the others. It was good these people didn't know what Ashar could do. At least, he *hoped* they didn't. Hopefully, they were still frantically searching the building for the other three kids. Hopefully, they were thinking to themselves, "*They couldn't have just disappeared out of thin air!*"

Ashar now witnessed a scene of chaos. Kareem, using his unique abilities, had grabbed everything within reach—papers, pens, clipboards—and plastered them to the men attempting to restrain him. He stuck items directly onto their faces, blinding them. In a particularly desperate move, he grabbed the fingers of two different guards and stuck them together, eliciting painful cries as they attempted to separate. Ashar cringed at the sight, dreading the gruesome aftermath of their eventual separation. Kareem's sticky abilities were powerful indeed.

However, Ashar doubted these abilities alone would suffice to free Kareem from this predicament. He realized he needed to intervene. Unseen by the guards, who were preoccupied with Kareem, Ashar had teleported right behind them.

It was time for a distraction.

Scanning the area frantically, he decided to mimic Kareem's tactics by grabbing any object he could find. Though he couldn't make items stick, he could still use them as projectiles. "Hey!" he yelled, hurling a coffee mug at one of the guards. "Let him go!"

Together, Kareem and Ashar hurled item after item, working tirelessly to free Kareem from his captors.

In a desperate move, Ashar picked up a glass beaker, unaware of its contents, and threw it at a guard who seemed to be pulling a small object from his pocket—a syringe, possibly—while another held Kareem back, a clipboard obscuring his face.

The beaker shattered against the guard's face, the liquid inside causing him to scream—either from a chemical burn or from shards of glass embedding in his skin. His agony provided the distraction needed; the other guard faltered, and Kareem wrenched free from their grasp.

"Over here!" Ashar shouted urgently, his voice tinged with anger born of sheer terror. He needed them to escape immediately. Kareem, panting heavily, rushed toward Ashar. Glancing back at the door, Ashar visualized the House of the Venari, opened it up, and just as another guard noticed their actions and charged at them, both Kareem and Ashar dove through. Kareem went head-first, and Ashar fell backward onto his foot, rolling to kick the door shut behind them, preventing the guard from following.

They had done it—they were free.

As they sat panting, trying to collect themselves, it didn't take long for them to realize something was amiss. They were inside Ovi and Kareem's room, but there shouldn't have been anyone else there except for Ashar and Kareem. Ashar was certain he had directed the rest of the team to other parts of the House of the Venari. So why were there three other figures in the room with them?

WHERE, came a deep, malevolent voice, *did you two just come from?*

Ashar stared up in horror at the three adults. By escaping into the room with Kareem, they had inadvertently barged in on Savar, Hessa, and even Zaid, who appeared as though they had just been in the midst of a discussion inside Kareem and Ovi's room.

This was not good at all.

CHAPTER 16
THE PRICE OF REBELLION

Kareem was just having a bad, *bad* dream. That had to be it. He would wake up from it any moment now. He didn't just barely escape with his freedom with the help of Ashar, and he didn't just get back into his room at the House of the Venari through a portal only to find three of the last people he wanted to see standing inside his bedroom.

And yet, there Savar, Hessa, and Zaid stood with faces of fury and astonishment.

Where was Zara? Ovi and Binita? He desperately wanted to ask Ashar if he had rescued them as well, but he couldn't in front of the adults.

Uh, hey there, Ashar said sheepishly to them, grabbing the back of his neck as he got to his feet. Kareem was stunned into silence. He couldn't even move off the floor yet. He didn't know what to do as he stared up at them. All he knew was that it was going to be really hard to explain his way out of this one. It was hard to even fathom trying to when he didn't know if his other friends were okay. What if SPE captured them? What if they were being imprisoned in the same place Neelan was right this very moment? What if SPE's people unleashed ubir to torment them?

Answer Savar's question, Hessa demanded. All three of the adults still looked furious. More than that. Bewildered. Almost in a wild, crazed sort of way. Kareem wondered how long they had been inside his bedroom. How long it took them to realize that he and the others on his team were missing. How much did they know about where Kareem and Ashar had just been? And why was Zaid with them? The fact that *he* was present was definitely not a good sign. Although Zaid was a Venari, he was Queen Kinza's consort. He was from the Grand Hall, which meant higher-ups knew about the situation, too.

Ashar and Kareem looked at each other, both of them unsure. But then Ashar bugged his eyes out at Kareem, and Kareem knew what that meant: as the team leader, Kareem had to be the one to answer the question. He wished he could talk it over with Ashar and the others first. That they could collectively come to an agreement about just how much they should tell Savar and them.

We can explain, he tried, knowing how stupid that sounded to start with. Savar didn't ask them to explain *why* they had been where they were; he wanted to know the facts. He wanted the answer he probably already knew. *All we want to do is get Neelan back home safe. His family! They're worried about him! They think he's dead!* He was desperate to make them see reason. To say the right thing that led to Savar allowing him to continue his explanation.

It was clear straight away to Kareem that he had said the wrong thing, however. Hessa momentarily buried her face in her hands. Zaid turned and took a few steps away from Kareem and Ashar, looking as though he were so angry he might punch something. Savar, on the other hand, held Kareem's gaze with a feverish intensity in his eyes, his hands on his hips, his stance strong and scary, especially with Kareem down there on the floor.

Stand up, you stupid boy, Savar snapped.

With a jolt, Kareem did as he was told.

What did we talk about? Savar asked. Kareem quickly realized he wasn't talking to him but to the other two adults. *We knew this would happen. We fully expected Kareem and his team to do something like this again.*

We shouldn't have resumed trusting them, Hessa said. *Not after their last stunt.*

You were foolish to give them another chance, Zaid barked, glowering in Kareem and Ashar's direction. Kareem hated disappointing someone he looked up to so much. He wanted to be like Zaid. Like Tejas.

His stomach rolled when he thought of his brother. Tejas. Had he heard? Did he know how much trouble his brother was in? How soon until the rest of his family knew?

This was almost too much for him to bear.

Kareem swallowed. *We just want to help.* He tried to sound strong. He didn't know if it was working.

We knew you'd do something like this again, so we've been watching you, Savar said venomously.

When you and Ashar and the rest of your team missed your classes today, I was notified at the Grand Hall, Zaid explained, turning back to them slowly, his fists balled.

Hey! You went through our stuff? Ashar asked, his tone suddenly angry. Almost angry enough that Kareem didn't quite recognize him. And he didn't understand why Ashar asked the question. None of them had said anything about going through their belongings. *Where did you get that?*

Kareem had to follow where Ashar's eyes were staring, and he saw it in Hessa's hand. In it, her long fingers were curved around a cell phone. *Their* cell phone.

And we were very right to, it would seem, Hessa replied coolly, not even looking ashamed of having done so. *This phone does not belong to you. I'm willing to bet I could find more if I talked to the others as well.*

Ashar clenched his jaw and stared at them. But Kareem didn't want to resign himself to being contempt and caught. He still wanted to try and find a way to get them out of this mess. To keep them from getting into any trouble. He felt foolish for making the others skip class that day. He knew it had been a huge risk to take and that there would be repercussions for skipping as it was, but he hoped that when their teachers talked to them later, they'd either be able to say that they had simply gone on an adventure around Rhapta. Either that, or Kareem hoped to be able to tell them that yes, they did leave Rhapta, which they knew they weren't supposed to do, but in doing so, they were able to save Neelan and all the other missing Anunnaki. Unfortunately, now he couldn't use either excuse.

Not only have we caught you teleporting, but we found your stolen smartphone. We searched the room and saw other documents that record your research from the past few weeks. Savar slowly shook his head. *I suggest you tell us everything you know. Down to the very last detail.*

I don't know, Kareem, Ashar said in a low voice. Kareem couldn't believe his audacity. The adults were standing right there. They could hear him. They could hear the way it sounded, as though Ashar didn't trust them enough to let them in on everything they had just witnessed. But they were Anunnaki. Venari. They were important people in Rhapta. Zaid was the queen's consort, for goodness' sake. Kareem thought it would be better to fill them in on everything they knew. If any information they divulged would help the adults have a better chance of finding Neelan and the other missing Anunnaki, he had to take it.

Okay. Kareem held out his hands to the adults in a calming manner. *We will. We will tell you everything.* And just like the last time, after they returned from Canada, Kareem told Savar everything. The only thing he left out was the rest of the team's involvement. As far as Savar, Hessa, Zaid, and everyone else at the House of the Venari had to know, Ashar and Kareem were the only ones who went on this adventure tonight.

Hessa snorted at that part. *You can't expect me to believe that.*

It's true, Ashar said. *They weren't with us. We didn't tell them about our plan. We figured that the more of us that knew, and the more of us that weren't, it would only draw more attention.*

Then why weren't they in their classes this morning? Zaid asked.

We sent them off on an errand in town. To get them off our trail. To protect them.

Kareem was impressed with Ashar's quick thinking.

I don't trust it, Zaid said.

Neither do I, Hessa agreed.

Savar sneered at Kareem and Ashar. *I'm almost positive the rest of the team was involved. But, as they are not in this room with us now, I dare say we have no proof. All we have is what is in front of us. The tangible members of the team who can receive their punishment.*

Sir, Kareem tried, *how can you be upset with us for trying to do the right thing? I get it was reckless, but we found out useful information. What about the animals? Peru? The transcripts between the Director and Tahir?*

You're foolish to think we were in the dark about all of that.

Well... Well... If you have all of this information, why aren't you doing anything about it?! Great. Kareem hadn't meant to lose his temper. But now he was in the same boat as Ashar. He knew it was useless; there was no point in trying to change these adults' minds.

We've already had this talk, Kareem, Savar said. *Because of you, SPE knows that we are onto them. Because of you, any plans we may or may not have made have been thwarted. You couldn't keep your nose out of our business, and not only do you have to pay the consequence, but I'm afraid so many others might have to as well.*

"No," Kareem whispered, thinking of Neelan. He pictured him in a small dark room, sitting in a corner, malnourished and dehydrated, hoping for rescue.

What are you going to do to us? Ashar asked darkly, looking up at Savar through lowered eyebrows.

Well, you may not recall this, Ashar, as you were not yet a part of the team the last time this particular group got into some trouble, but I strictly stated that the punishment for leaving Rhapta would be—why don't you finish the question, Kareem?

Imprisonment, Kareem uttered, not looking at anyone. He expected Ashar to yell at him. To be angry that he didn't know the extent of the consequences that could be given to them if they were caught.

Savar sighed. *And here I thought Ashar would help keep you all out of trouble. I thought you wouldn't want him to know about your business and that you'd treat him like an outsider. I thought you'd stray from breaking any rules in fear of him knowing. In fear of thinking that he was in ties with me and would tell me everything.*

Now it made sense. The answer Savar had given him before about why he put Ashar on Kareem's team had been a complete lie. It was for his own self-serving purposes. Kareem should have known.

Well then, Hessa said, lifting her chin up authoritatively. *For now, you're confined to this room. Even you, Ashar. Consider this your temporary holding cell. There will be someone posted outside at all times until your punishment is finally ready to be given.*

ULTIMATELY, it was decided that not just one but two warriors were needed to keep an eye on Kareem and Ashar. Ovi was no longer allowed inside of his shared bedroom, at least temporarily. Ashar felt bad about that, but he figured it was a small price to pay, all things considered. At least Ovi wasn't going to be punished alongside them. Zaid or Savar had apparently decided they needed the second warrior to be on the inside of the bedroom, keeping a watchful eye on Ashar to make sure he didn't use the bedroom door to teleport the boys out of there once again. So, while Kareem and Ashar awaited their punishment, they couldn't even really talk to one another. Not about anything important. Not about anything that happened in the SPE headquarters. How they had been tracked. Set up. No wonder there had never been any alarms. No wonder everything seemed so easy to grant access to. It was like SPE *wanted* them to know what they were up to—to an extent. But why? Get them interested enough so that when the guards rained down upon them, they were too distracted to get away quickly enough?

Ashar was left to his own thoughts. He knew things were going to be so much worse this time. He knew he couldn't get in trouble like this and not be expelled. All he could hope for now was that the adults wouldn't actually go forward with the imprisonment. They were just kids! Just stupid, young kids!

Maybe Kareem was able to get some sleep, for he looked very still over on his bed every time Ashar rolled over yet again and checked on him. Ashar, on the other hand, didn't feel like he would ever sleep again. Waiting for the punishment—it was torture. He had Nasrin to think about. His uncle. He had to provide for his uncle. He was the only one who could!

It felt good being a part of Kareem's team at the beginning. But of course, Ashar didn't really think about the consequences of getting caught until it was too late. Here they were, with nothing to show for the risks they had taken. Neelan was still missing, and Anunnaki were still being hunted. Every day, more and more of them were going to keep going missing. Ashar had been hoping to be a hero. But now, he was being seen as a villain.

Ashar wasn't sure how long exactly went by before a knock sounded on the door. When the warrior standing guard from the inside opened it, the warrior on the outside stalked his way in, looking very straight-faced.

What's happened? Kareem asked immediately, bolting up in bed. Ashar was desperate to know, too. It was agonizing to wait a second longer. At least once he knew what his punishment was, he could figure out the next step.

I have come to tell you you are under arrest. And you are to be brought to the underground prisons.

Underground? Ashar shivered. *That's where they keep the ubir.*

Both of the warriors looked indifferent. *It's just the orders I was given,* the first one said.

We're actually getting arrested? Kareem asked, looking younger than Ashar had ever seen him. At the same time, there was something about his eyes that aged him. It was like all of the hopes and dreams he had before arriving at the House of the Venari had vanished from them. He lost his sparkle and determination. Ashar felt guilty about it. Being older than the rest of his team, he could've acted as a mentor figure, similar to Neelan. All of the other teams in the House still had their mentors. The other four in their group hadn't had anyone to guide them all this time. But Ashar could've done so, and instead, he fed into their delusions, not realizing that 'delusion' was what to call it.

How long do we have to stay there? Ashar asked. He wondered if Kareem would be okay in a place like the underground prison. He wondered if he, himself, would be able to find a way to teleport himself out of there.

From what I was told, you are to go to trial, the warrior messenger said. *You are to face the queen. It seems all of the Rhaptan government has found out how much danger you two put Rhapta in. That place you went, those headquarters of that group, it's likely they have clear documentation of everything that went down that evening.*

You are a bunch of idiots, really, the second warrior said, crossing his arms over his bulky chest. It was strange to hear him talk. He had stayed intensely silent this entire time. *It's not even my place to make a comment, but with a kid of my own, I have a hideous need to remind you what a huge mistake you've made. How you've threatened the very safety of our species. As for me? I hope your punishment is a great one. You boys are a disgrace to Rhapta.*

Ashar knew he would never be able to forget this moment.

He and Kareem were escorted out of the bedroom, their arms pinned to their sides by laqueus. This special rope, painful to kids and mildly annoying to adults, bound Anunnaki abilities. It was tied around them as the warriors guided them down the halls of the House of the Venari. It felt as though he was moving in slow motion. The shame he felt inside of him. The fear. The worry. And it was like he wore it for everyone to see. There were other pupils and Venari everywhere, watching the scene unfold and looking at Kareem and Ashar with a mixture of shock and horror on their faces. There were whispers. There were muttered insults that Ashar couldn't quite make out. The warrior's words replayed in his mind, and he couldn't get it to stop.

He was a disgrace to Rhapta. What would his uncle think?

RESILIENT HEARTS

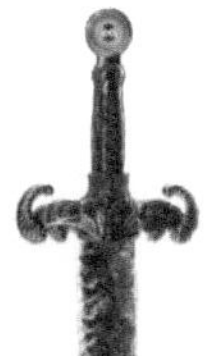

In the deep underbelly of an ominous underground prison, Kareem sat opposite Ashar, the dim light from torches flickering against the damp stone walls. The two teenagers were confined in a small cell, heavy iron bars separating them from the long, echoing corridor, at the end of which lay a spiral staircase winding up into darkness, its end invisible, reminding Kareem just how far underground they really were. The same laqueus that had bound them on their journey here was also embedded into the walls of these cells, so their abilities were severely dampened.

Kareem eyed Ashar, who sat with his head bent and his elbows on his knees on a stone bench across from him. They had been silent for a while. But Kareem couldn't hold his figurative tongue or be left to his own thoughts any longer, despite it looking like *talking* was the last thing Ashar wanted to do, based on his state.

I can't believe I let this happen, Kareem muttered inside his head, wondering if he said it loud enough internally for Ashar to be able to hear him. He almost wanted to talk out loud, just to fill some of the silence. To ease the worry that he'd hear groans or growls from ubir in nearby cells. His eyes were fixed on the flames emitting from the torch on the wall outside their cell. *Just trying to help Neelan, and now this...*

Ashar looked over at him, his expression unreadable in the flickering light. *It's not like we had many options,* he responded, his tone flat. *We did what we thought was right.*

Kareem shifted uncomfortably. How was he supposed to get used to this? This couldn't be his new reality. He couldn't accept that he was stuck in here. That the trial with Queen Kinza might not go well, and he and Ashar could suffer a terrible fate...

Kareem wasn't used to making apologies; it was a rare occurrence that he found himself regretting his decisions. Yet, sitting here, it weighed heavily on him that everything that happened had been his fault. When he spoke again, he kept his voice low and avoided Ashar's eye contact. He couldn't bear to see the blame on his face. *Look, I'm sorry for getting you into this mess. You were right the other day when you said we needed to come up with a better, more thought-out plan.*

Ashar waved a hand. *I was only saying that because I was trying to distract you guys from the fact that I was worried my abilities would fail you all.*

Still. Kareem sighed and leaned back, pressing his back against the damp stone wall. *Making the decision to cut class—I should have known it would immediately put the spotlight on us.*

Ashar's response came slowly, his eyes meeting Kareem's. *We're in this together, right?* His voice was even, almost too calm, and it left Kareem questioning the sincerity of his words. Ashar couldn't possibly forgive him. It felt too easy.

Still, Kareem nodded, though the doubt lingered. Ashar's forgiveness seemed too swift, too smooth to be entirely genuine. Maybe Kareem was just deflecting. Maybe he thought things were suspicious because, had he been in Ashar's shoes, he wouldn't be so quick to forgive. They sat in silence for a while as Kareem thought about this. He somewhat hoped Ashar would eventually have something else to say. Maybe words that would offer Kareem more comfort.

Their shared silence was interrupted by the sound of heavy footsteps descending the staircase. The rhythmic thuds of boots on stone grew louder, and both teens looked toward the sound. Kareem got to his feet, too filled with anticipation to sit still, too full of dread.

Two figures appeared, bringing more light with them, for they carried two more lit torches of their own. One of them, a broad-shouldered man with a stern face, approached their cell. He carried a large ring of keys, their metallic clinking resonating in the quiet.

Stopping in front of the cell, the warrior looked between Kareem and Ashar. *You've been granted permission to see some visitors,* he announced. He selected a key and inserted it into the lock, a heavy click emitting.

Hope filled Kareem. He hadn't thought he'd be allowed to speak to anyone except for Ashar until the trial. Even Ashar seemed glad about the news; he got to his feet as well and rushed to stand by Kareem's side.

The door creaked open.

Kareem and Ashar were led out of the dark, damp confines of the underground prison into the blinding brightness of the day. Kareem squinted in the sunlight, not used to it after having been in the dim underground.

Who came to speak to us? Kareem asked the men. Naturally, neither answered. Kareem and Ashar shared a look, and Ashar shrugged. He didn't seem worried, but Kareem feared it was going to be Savar, Zaid, or one of their teachers there to keep yelling at them or to let them know they had been expelled. Or what if it was Kareem's parents and someone from Ashar's family? What if Kareem and Ashar were about to get the lecture of a lifetime and be forced to see the disappointment etched across their families' faces?

The teens were brought to an open field, where an old stone table rested under the open sky. Thankfully, Binita, Zara, and Ovi were waiting for them, perking up when Kareem and Ashar came into sight.

The warriors stopped walking, so Kareem and Ashar did as well; Kareem was unsure how close he was allowed to get to his visitors, and he didn't want to break any more rules.

At least not right now.

We will be keeping a close watch on you both. Don't even think of trying anything, one of the men said.

With a sigh of relief, Kareem approached the table, Ashar in tow. Their friends didn't exactly look happy to see them. But Kareem knew that wasn't the case. He knew this just wasn't the time for smiling or pleasantries.

They took their seats, Kareem breathing in as much fresh air as he could.

Zara immediately reached across the table, her gesture stopped only by the sharp glance of a nearby warrior. Kareem stared at her hand for a lingering moment, wondering which of the two of them she had meant to reach for.

It's brave, what you did, Binita said, sounding full of admiration. *And just for the record, we* weren't *involved in what happened at SPE.* Her eyes flickered to the warriors with a hint of mischief.

Kareem nodded, appreciating her effort to keep things light. *Thanks, B. I just wish there was more we could do now.*

Zara, tapping her fingers impatiently on the stone, interjected sharply, *You shouldn't have taken all the blame.* Then she quieted her tone so only they could hear. *We* were *all there. It's not just on you two.* She sounded angry, which made Kareem almost smile because it was so typical of her. They saved her from being tossed into a terrible dark place, and she was *mad* at them.

Ovi, sitting quietly beside Zara, seemed lost in thought, his gaze distant. Kareem was used to him being the most introspective of the group, but now, more than ever, he wanted his close friend to say something.

The conversation shifted as Binita straightened up and let out a sorrowful sigh. *Do you two recall that creature Zara and I found back at SPE's headquarters?* Kareem did remember the bug-eyed weasel. He and Ashar nodded. *I was keeping it in our room,* Binita said, a certain note in her tone as though she were daydreaming about her new friend right then and there. But then her face fell slightly. *But Zara left the window open, and it escaped.*

Zara rolled her eyes, though she did look apologetic. *I didn't think it would actually leave,* she muttered. *That thing loved Binita.*

I couldn't have it go to the bathroom with me! Binita whined, though she didn't sound too upset with her roommate. Binita was quick to be forgiving.

I'm sorry that happened, Ashar said, pursing his lips into a straight line.

Binita rested an elbow on the table and put her chin in her hand. *I'm not even sure if it can survive on its own out here. I hadn't even figured out what it likes to eat yet. I'm sure he's starving and scared. Poor guy. And who's going to pet him? Or even worse! What if someone does come across him and pet him, and he begins to glow? What if the Rhaptan government gets its hands on him? My poor, cuddly boy.*

Kareem listened, a faint smile breaking through his concerns as he imagined the odd, wide-eyed creature scurrying around their room. He knew Binita was sad about it, but he couldn't help himself. It was moments like these—Binita's strange discoveries and quirky attitude, Zara's fiery spirit, and Ovi's thoughtful silences—that he had missed during his short time away from them. They were a team. They were supposed to be together. Ashar and Kareem didn't belong in that dreadful underground cell. They belonged with the three teens sitting across from them.

The group fell silent, and as they all sat under the open sky around the ancient stone table, a gentle breeze stirred the air. For a moment, things felt peaceful to Kareem. Hopeful, even. The harshness of their dungeon seemed a world away. Maybe things could still work out.

Ovi, always the one to hold the most worry and concern, leaned forward. His eyes had a strange, unfamiliar fierceness about them as he scanned the faces of his friends. *What do you all think is happening back at the SPE lab?* he asked. *With all those reports... the animals... the fact that we're pretty sure they set us up and wanted us to snoop around... What are they planning? It has to be more than just hunting Anunnaki and taking them off the streets like they're some sort of virus that must be eradicated.*

Binita, who had been observing a small ant making its way across the table, looked up, her brow furrowed in thought. *I'm not sure, but it's something big,* she replied. *Something that our teachers, the people who are supposed to be leading us, are choosing to ignore.*

Zara sighed deeply and intertwined her fingers, pressing them tightly together as she spoke. *It's horrible that you guys were caught. I wish there was more we could do. But with you both awaiting trial?* Her voice softened, full of worry. *I just... What about Neelan? What will happen to him?*

Ashar shook his head. *Don't think like that, Zar. We have to keep hope. Neelan's a Venari. He's strong—he'll be okay,* he said. But he sounded as though he was trying greatly to sound confident.

Yet, Zara's next words cut down all and any false optimism. *This isn't good. I... I can't help but feel like something massive is coming. Something so significant that none of us are prepared for it. SPE is planning something terrible. Tell me I am not alone in feeling this way.*

The group fell into another silence, this time a more uneasy one. Kareem watched as each member seemed lost in their own thoughts. Kareem did agree with Zara's speculation. He just didn't understand her sense of total hopelessness.

So, Kareem finally broke the silence. *If SPE is brewing something*

this big, shouldn't we be trying to find out more, do something about it?
He knew very well that the others were looking at him like his eyes
had suddenly grown to be the same size as Binita's weasel friend.

No one responded to him.

Kareem sighed. *We can't just give up,* he declared firmly.

But...Kareem, Zara chided. *You're in prison. We've been caught!
What else can we possibly do?*

Yes, Ashar and I are locked up, Kareem replied, *and yes, things look
grim. We're facing a trial before Queen Kinza. But that doesn't mean it's
the end.*

You are something else, Binita commented with a grin of disbelief at him. Zara's gaze at Kareem, however, remained skeptical.

*And what exactly do you propose we do from here, then, Kareem?
How can we even think about rescuing Neelan now with practically
every eye in Rhapta on us?*

Kareem refused to lose his determination. He refused to give
up. He needed to rally with the others to get him to feel the same
way he did. And he would. It would take some work. A lot of
convincing and even more careful planning. But as far as Kareem
saw it, they were already in as much trouble as they could get
themselves in. What did they have to lose now?

While Ashar, Zara, Ovi, and Binita all stared at their team
leader with careful eyes, Kareem took a deep breath, and then he
voiced the bold plan that had been forming in his mind ever since
the moment he returned from SPE's facility. *By going to Peru.*

EPILOGUE

The bright fluorescent lights of the SPE research facility's laboratory cast a harsh glow on the array of monitors aligned against the far wall. Each screen flickered and beeped with clinical indifference, displaying a recorded feed from dozens of different cameras hidden within the facility. The air was full of the sterile scent of antiseptics and cold metal. Wires sprawled across steel tables, connecting one ominous-looking instrument to another. The Director stood, his white hair practically glowing in the light of the screens in the room's otherwise shadowy darkness.

With a close gaze, he surveyed the footage looping on the central screen—a recent recount of five certain Anunnaki children. A small, grim smile creased his lips as he observed them making their escape from the dozens of men he had sent to capture them over at his staged facility. His eyes reflected the flickering images of one of the boys, the tall one, appearing out of random doors, rescuing his friend, and then reappearing to rescue more.

"Remarkable, isn't it?" The Director's voice was deep and ominous over the hum of machinery. His two assistants, clad in pristinely white lab coats, nodded, their faces as impassive as the walls enclosing them.

"Yes, sir. The abilities these kids seem to possess may be more superior than we projected," his favorite assistant, a young woman with quick thinking and no time for error, remarked, tapping a few keys on a keyboard, causing one of the other screens to zoom in on Tahir, who was gaunt and pallid-faced on the monitor. His cheekbones were sharply defined, his face horribly sunken in, showing how much he had endured during his time with them.

"And this one," his right-hand man—technically *woman*—pointed out, "is able to endure more than we projected as well."

"That subject has endurance, yes, but to be honest with you, it's the resilience of his spirit that intrigues me the most," the Director mused, clasping his hands behind his back as he temporarily moved away from the footage of the kids to the live feed of Tahir in his confinements. "To withstand such... rigorous procedures and still cling to life..." There was an almost unreadable excitement in his tone. In all truth, the Director thrived on men like Tahir. On naive kids like those they lured into the facility.

After a moment of silent contemplation, the Director turned on his heel, his lab coat swirling around him. "Come," he commanded sharply, and his assistants followed. They descended deeper into the facility, past metal doors with various symbols on them, to a heavily fortified room at the end of a long hallway. The door was massive, made of iron, and designed to withstand any attempts to escape or rescue. Pressing his fingerprint to the screen on the pad next to the door, the door swung open with a loud, metallic groan, and the Director granted them all access to its interior.

Inside, the cell was barely lit by a single bulb, allowing for plenty of shadowy corners. Tahir was there, lying on a thin mattress that the Director knew couldn't be the least bit comfortable. He figured Tahir might as well sleep on the concrete floor. Sometimes, Tahir did just that.

Now, Tahir looked worse for wear. His eyes used to hold fire and passion. Now, they were dull. Now, they didn't even glance at the Director or his assistants as they approached.

"Mr. Tahir, how good of you to still be with us," the Director began, his voice full of fake warmth as he approached the tired, sick man. "Your contributions to our research have been... *invaluable.*"

Tahir let out a weak, raspy laugh that was devoid of humor. "Are you here to kill me now?" Even the effort of speaking caused him to grimace.

"*Kill* you? Oh, no, Tahir, you are far too useful for that," the Director replied with a thin smile. "In fact, I am here to thank you. You've allowed us to achieve far more than we ever thought possible." He crouched beside Tahir, observing him like a fascinating insect. "Imagine, Tahir, a world where human limitations are but a distant memory. You've helped pave the way for that new horizon. Isn't that something?"

"A world built on agony," he whispered, his voice hoarse. "Rhapta needs to fall. Not be blended in with your kind, allowed to be seen as useful. You're making a grave mistake."

"I think that's a matter of perspective," the Director said, standing back up. "It would be wasteful to get rid of them. To not use what your kind can provide. You've become part of something greater than yourself. Don't you see how beautiful it is to be a sacrifice for the greater good of humanity?" It was a rhetorical question, and thankfully, Tahir seemed to catch on to that.

Leaving Tahir in the dim glow of his cell, the Director stepped out, and his assistants followed. As the iron door slammed shut, sealing Tahir in once again, the Director's thoughts had already moved on to what was still to come.

Back in the lab, the Director paused by the computers and turned to his assistants, a small smile forming on his lips. "Ensure that Tahir's condition is stable enough to proceed. We can't afford to lose him—not when we are this close to the pinnacle of our achievements."

The assistants nodded, their faces professionally blank, just how the Director liked it. As they dispersed to carry out his orders, the Director stayed by the computers, watching the replay of Tahir's latest session. He closely dissected every reaction and response captured by the high-definition cameras. The Director felt something like a god among men.

Knowledge was power, after all.

DRAMATIS PERSONAE

Recruits

Kareem Maamoum – Team leader and younger brother to Tejas

Zara al-Hamzi – Kareem's teammate and rival

Ovi Fadel – Kareem's teammate and roommate

Binita Chudasama – Kareem's teammate and Zara's roommate

Ashar Kouri - Kareem's new teammate

Caden El Tain – A venari pupil

Idris Lajami – A venari pupil

Faiza Shahd – Friend of Zara and Inaam's roommate

Inaam Kirdar – Friend of Zara and Faiza's roommate

Veer – A venari pupil

Aryan – Younger brother of Waqas

Samira – A venari pupil

Jalla – A venari pupil

Tarun Munir – A venari pupil

Mira – A venari pupil

Kareem's Family

Tejas Maamoum – Kareem's elder brother and venari

Akilah Maamoum – Kareem's young sister

Some of the Venari
Savar Basu – Head of the Venari
Zaid Hatem – Apprentice to Savar and the Queen's Consort
Hessa Darvish – Physical combat instructor
Amol Khanna – Assistant physical training instructor
Laban Dayal – Mental conditioning instructor
Tala – Abilities instructor
Afif – Human studies instructor
Neelan Qureshi – Mentor to Keelan's team
Waqas – A new venari and elder brother of Aryan
Wael – Friend of Waqas

Ummanu
Bahati – Watches over the portal in Moshi
Adam – Watched over the portal in Toronto

GLOSSARY OF TERMS

abilities *(ah bill it ees) n.* Powers that each Anunnaki has. The abilities vary per person and are supernatural in nature.

Anunnaki *(ahn new nock ee) n.* A species thought to have originated from Rhapta to guide humanity. They live longer than humans, can speak to each other telepathically, and have abilities. They reside only in Rhapta. If an Anunnaki leaves the city limits, their abilities fade, and they slowly become human and forget Rhapta. Some live outside the city limits but still within the psychic barrier. Their abilities are weakened, and they have developed a need for verbal speech.

Elder *(ell der) n.* One of the fifty leaders of Rhapta. One out of every fifty is a Grand Elder who leads in ceremony and prophecy.

guakal *(gwa kall) n.* A fist-sized, rigid-shelled, lime-green fruit with miniature red spikes on its exterior; native to Rhapta.

laqueus *(la kwees) n.* A rope, silvery-gray in color, made by Anunnaki used to bind or dampen abilities. Mildly annoying to Anunnaki, physically painful to humans.

magalkan'a *(muh gal kahn uh) n.* Commonly known as Aurastone, believed to be the origin of Anunnaki abilities. Shades range from white to azure.

mark *(mar k) n.* The tribal tattoo that every Anunnaki is born with. Only *venari* and ubir have different tattoos. *Venari's* are larger and need to be reapplied monthly; it allows them to enter the human world while retaining their abilities for a short time. Ubir tattoos are similar but red and swollen, as if infected.

reykalkan'o *(ray kal kon oh) n.* Commonly known as Deathstone. It is cracked Aurastone. Created either by blood magic, or taking it from Rhapta. Its presence is extremely painful to Anunnaki, creating a high-pitched ringing. If the Anunnaki cannot hear it, it's unlikely to be harmful.

Rhapta *(rap tuh) n.* An ancient city located near Mt. Kilimanjaro. It is hidden behind a psychic barrier and unknown to humanity. Currently at half capacity due to its dwindling population.

ubir *(oo beer) n.* Anunnaki that have defected from Rhapta and turned to blood magic to exist outside of the city while retaining their abilities. They quickly become rabid and need to sacrifice humans to retain their abilities. Their Aura is chaotic and painful.

Ummanu *(oo mon oo) n.* Humans who are aware of Anunnaki's existence and have allied with them. Most watch over the portals around the world.

venari *(venn are ee) n.* Anunnaki bounty hunters tasked with locating and returning ubir from human society. They are shunned within Rhapta due to their "dirty" work and closeness with human society.

Author's Note

Dear Beloved Reader,

Thank you so much for reading *Shadows of Rhapta*, book two of the Rhaptaverse Chronicles. We hope you enjoyed the adventures and the addition of Ashar from the team. If you've read *Portal Magic*, you might have recognized Ashar from that story. Book three is in the works, so make sure you sign up for my mailing list or follow my author profile on your chosen book platform to be notified of its release. Visit my website (LilySkyy.com) to be the first to know about new releases and special happenings such as previews and give-a-ways!

Again, I thank you for reading, and I can't wait to join you on the next adventure!

Sincerely,

Lily Skyy

ALSO BY LILY SKYY

THE HIDDEN PROPHECY SERIES

Book 1: Cryptic Magic

Book 2: Erratic Magic

Book 3: Infinite Magic

Book 4: Corrupt Magic

THE RHAPTAVERSE CHRONICLES

(sequel to The Hidden Prophecy)

Prequel Novella: Portal Magic

Book 1: Rise of the Venari

Book 2: Shadows of Rhapta

THE UNLIKELY DEFENDERS SERIES

Book 1: The Unchosen Ones

Book 2: The Unfavorable Heroes

Book 3: The Unlucky Guardians

Book 4: The Unseemly Protectors

Book 5: The Untimely Champions